481· W9-CHH-387

The Demon in the Teahouse

Dorothy Hoobler
AR B.L.: 5.3
Points: 6.0

The eyes of the demon

As he tried to get up, something strange happened. The house seemed to turn on its side. Seikei puzzled over it for a moment. Then he realized it was not the house, but he who had toppled over. He was lying on the soft ground, and had spilled the tea.

The tea. He realized too late that the tea was what had caused him to become relaxed. So relaxed that now he could no longer move.

A face appeared in front of him. Eyes looked directly into his. He recognized them, and then fear took hold of him.

This must be the way a true samurai feels, he thought, when he faces an enemy in mortal combat. He closed his eyes.

"Details of shogun-era Japan are seamlessly woven into a gripping story."   —*The Horn Book*

"A fast-paced mystery with a well-constructed plot that moves quickly and often in dramatic ways."
                                        —*School Library Journal*

"This is a traditional mystery, with a well-conceived plot, authentic clues, and a satisfying conclusion."
                                        —*Booklist*

OTHER BOOKS YOU MAY ENJOY

The Demon in the Teahouse

DOROTHY & THOMAS HOOBLER

SLEUTH
PUFFIN

PUFFIN BOOKS

Published by the Penguin Group

Penguin Young Readers Group, 345 Hudson Street, New York, New York 10014, U.S.A.

Penguin Group (Canada), 10 Alcorn Avenue, Toronto, Ontario, Canada M4V 3B2
(a division of Pearson Penguin Canada Inc.)

Penguin Books Ltd, 80 Strand, London WC2R 0RL, England

Penguin Ireland, 25 St Stephen's Green, Dublin 2, Ireland
(a division of Penguin Books Ltd)

Penguin Group (Australia), 250 Camberwell Road, Camberwell,
Victoria 3124, Australia (a division of Pearson Australia Group Pty Ltd)

Penguin Books India Pvt Ltd, 11 Community Centre, Panchsheel Park,
New Delhi - 110 017, India

Penguin Group (NZ), Cnr Airborne and Rosedale Roads, Albany, Auckland 1310,
New Zealand (a division of Pearson New Zealand Ltd)

Penguin Books (South Africa) (Pty) Ltd, 24 Sturdee Avenue,
Rosebank, Johannesburg 2196, South Africa

Registered Offices: Penguin Books Ltd, 80 Strand, London WC2R 0RL, England

First published in the United States of America by Philomel Books,
a division of Penguin Putnam Books for Young Readers, 2001

Published by Puffin Books, a division of Penguin Putnam Books for Young Readers, 2002

This Sleuth edition published by Puffin Books,
a division of Penguin Young Readers Group, 2006

1 2 3 4 5 6 7 8 9 10

THE LIBRARY OF CONGRESS HAS CATALOGED THE PHILOMEL EDITION AS FOLLOWS:

Hoobler, Dorothy.

The demon in the teahouse / Dorothy and Thomas Hoobler.

p.   cm.

Sequel to: The ghost in the Tokaido Inn

Summary: In eighteenth-century Japan, fourteen-year-old Seikei, a merchant's son in
training to become a samurai, helps his patron investigate a series of murders and arson
in the capital city of Edo, each of which is associated in some way with a popular geisha.

ISBN: 0-399-23499-3 (hc)

1. Japan—History—Tokugawa period, 1600–1868—Juvenile fiction.
[1. Japan—History—Tokugawa period, 1600–1868—Fiction. 2. Geishas—Fiction.
3. Samurai—Fiction. 4. Ooka, Tadasuke, 1677?–1751?—Fiction.
5. Mystery and detective stories.] I. Hoobler, Thomas. II. Title.
PZ7.H6227De 2001   [Fic]—dc21   00-050184   CIP

Puffin Books ISBN 0-14-240540-X

Printed in the United States of America

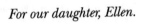

For our daughter, Ellen.

CONTENTS

PREFACE

Nearly three centuries ago, the largest city in the world was Edo, the headquarters of Japan's military government. There, in a huge stone castle, lived the *shogun* Yoshimune, the eighth member of the Tokugawa family to rule Japan.

The first Tokugawa shogun, Ieyasu, had seized power by defeating his enemies in battle. His descendants knew that they might lose their power if they allowed rivals to become too strong. The shogun's palace was surrounded by a network of rivers and moats designed to protect it against attack. Furthermore, the shogun required all his *daimyos,* or lords, to spend every other year in Edo, where he could keep a close eye on them. He appointed officials whose only task was to spy on others.

Like all the members of Japan's upper class, the Tokugawas were hereditary warriors, or *samurai.* Trained from birth in all the military skills, samurai also prided themselves on their artistic appreciation. A properly trained samurai was expected to be skilled at flower arranging, conducting the elaborate tea ceremony, and writing poetry.

A true samurai followed a code of honor and devotion to his lord. Normally, a samurai was trained from birth for the role he or she would play in life. Under unusual circumstances, a person from one of the lower classes might be adopted into a samurai family. Such a person was fourteen-year-old Seikei, born the son of a merchant in the city of Osaka. Through bravery, skill, and luck, Seikei had carried out a task set for him by Judge Ooka, one of the shogun's most trusted officials. In return, the childless judge adopted Seikei as his son. Now, however, Seikei had to live up to the challenge.

1—
THE SECRET OF KYUDO

eikei stood facing the target with his bow held ready. He fitted the notch of the arrow into the heavy string of the bow. As he pulled the arrow into shooting position, his arms strained with the effort of bending the bow while keeping it steady. Feeling the blood pounding at his temples, he took a deep breath, sighted down the shaft of the arrow, and released it.

It flew through the air as swiftly as a bird heading for its nest at twilight, and pierced the center of the demon's head on the target.

At least, that was the way Seikei had imagined it when he was a merchant's son and had watched samurai warriors practicing their archery. Then, it had looked easy. But the first time Seikei tried it, the arrow wobbled like a leaf falling from a tree. It not only missed the target; it never even got that far.

That had been two weeks ago, and Seikei had shown little improvement since then. Bunzo, his teacher, had been patient. Seikei knew it wasn't out of kindness. Bunzo was showing respect for his lord, Judge Ooka, who had adopted Seikei and given him the chance to learn the skills of a samurai.

Slowly, Bunzo again went through each of the eight steps in shooting an arrow. Seikei tried to imitate him at each step, but Bunzo shook his head.

"What am I doing wrong?" Seikei asked.

Bunzo took a deep breath. Seikei knew that was meant to suppress his anger.

"You are thinking," Bunzo said.

Seikei hung his head. It was true. He was concentrating so hard on doing each step that he couldn't do them properly.

"A samurai must possess the way of the warrior," Bunzo lectured Seikei.

Seikei finished the lesson in his own mind: "Not watch, but become. Not think, but be." If Seikei thought about what he was doing, he would never be able to do it well. *Kyudo*—the art of archery—was not merely a physical skill, to be learned. It was a way of thinking.

"It may come to you with practice," said Bunzo. But he didn't sound hopeful.

"How long did you have to practice," asked Seikei, "before you mastered kyudo?"

"I drew my first bow at the age of three," said Bunzo. "But I did not shoot an arrow till I was nearly four." He glowered at Seikei. "You do not have that much time."

Seikei understood. For the first thirteen years of his

life, he had been the son of a tea merchant. That meant his destiny was to become a merchant in his turn. In time, his own children would become merchants. That was the proper order of things. Everyone is born into his or her own place: as a samurai, a farmer, an artisan, or—lowest of all—a merchant, one who merely sells what others create. That is the proper order of things, and to disturb order is to risk destroying everything.

Yet Seikei yearned to be a samurai. A foolish dream, he knew. But from the time he was very young, he had filled his head with the great deeds that samurai had done in the past. From books he taught himself the samurai ideals, and he even composed poetry, as noble samurai like the great Basho had done.

And then . . . the *kami,* the gods, blessed Seikei in a most startling way. He had witnessed a crime—or really, part of a crime. When Judge Ooka came to investigate the theft of a precious jewel, he had found Seikei's information to be useful. The judge had tested him further, sending him on a mission to find the thief.

It had been dangerous, but Seikei had accomplished the task. The judge declared him worthy, and made him a samurai in the only way possible: by adopting him as his own son.

Seikei's father, the merchant, had been surprised, but hardly displeased. He had seen no profit in a son who preferred writing poetry to the buying and selling of tea. Indeed, Seikei's younger brother, Hachi, had seemed far more able to take over the family business. Father had even been willing to make a suitable gift—a box of fine tea—to seal the bargain.

And Seikei's training began. To fail now would be to prove that it was indeed impossible for a merchant's son to rise to the rank of a samurai. Worse, it would shame Judge Ooka. The only honorable thing for Seikei to do, having disgraced his patron, would of course be to commit *seppuku,* to kill himself.

"Remove the target," Bunzo ordered.

Startled from his thoughts, Seikei wasn't sure he understood. "I am ready to continue practicing," he said.

"So you shall," said Bunzo. "For now, go and bring the target back here."

Seikei walked gingerly toward the cylinder of pressed straw that stood on the practice field. Bunzo had attached a drawing of a fierce-looking demon on it to encourage Seikei. It had horns, blood-red eyes, and a toothsome grimace that seemed to mock Seikei's efforts.

The back of Seikei's neck prickled as he wondered if Bunzo had decided to save the judge's honor himself. Seikei knew that an arrow from Bunzo's powerful bow would not miss—indeed, it would pass straight through any part of Seikei's body that it hit.

He took a deep breath and forced himself not to look back. If death came, a samurai should accept it calmly, he reminded himself. Honor was more important, because death will come to each person someday no matter what. If today Seikei was destined to die, he would die doing his duty.

However, when he reached the target in safety, he exhaled deeply, relieved to be alive. Bunzo had apparently decided there was still hope for him.

Seikei picked up the straw demon, which was tied together with two thin ropes. Had the demon been real, Seikei knew, he would have been gobbled up by it long before any of his arrows had any effect.

He carried the target back to where Bunzo stood waiting. Bunzo motioned for Seikei to pick up his bow and resume his stance. "Now," Bunzo said, "begin again."

Seikei slipped the notch of an arrow onto the bowstring once again. His right hand, enclosed in a three-fingered glove with a piece of buffalo horn protecting the thumb, pulled back the string. He could pull the bow a little farther than when he began training. But preparing to aim, he gazed out at the empty field.

"What am I to shoot at?" he asked.

"Nothing," said Bunzo. "Just shoot."

Seikei turned his head slightly, making sure the arrow was on a line with his mouth. He pulled the string until his arm hurt, and then released. He remembered to pause afterward, allowing the arrow to go on its proper course.

It seemed to go a bit farther this time, though of

course there was no target. Bunzo nodded. "Again," he said.

Seikei continued until ten arrows had left his bow. "Now go and pick up the arrows," Bunzo said.

Seikei obeyed, but when Bunzo commanded him to begin shooting the arrows again, he said, "I do not understand what I am supposed to be doing."

Bunzo's eyebrows rose, and he took another deep breath. "You do not have to understand," he said with a rasp in his voice.

Seikei nodded meekly. That was true. As a student, his duty was to obey. The point of the lesson, if there was one, would become clear later. Or he might never know what the point was. It did not matter. Learning the lesson was the goal.

Bunzo took the arrows from Seikei's hand. Swiftly, he shot all of them into the field again. He hardly paused between shots. It was very impressive. Seikei had read of the great feats of samurai archers of the past. He recalled Masatoki, who was said to have shot more than ten thousand arrows in a single day, hitting the target with each one.

"Now go and see where the arrows are," said Bunzo. Seikei walked into the field. He found all ten of the arrows in the same place, lying on top of one another. A tingle went down his back, and when he returned, he bowed deeply before Bunzo. "I could never become a master like you," said Seikei.

Bunzo did not seem pleased by the compliment. "In the first place," he replied, "I am not a master. Someday, when you see a master, you will know that. In the second place, if you tell yourself you will never be a master, then you are already defeated."

Bunzo pointed to the arrows Seikei carried. "Those should be part of you, as the bow should be part of your arm. Stay here and shoot them. Once, you had legs and did not know how to walk. Then you learned. It is the same with kyudo."

Seikei stayed on the practice field for the rest of the day. He thought of Masatoki's 10,000 arrows, but he himself shot only 820 before darkness fell. Even then, since there was no target, he would have continued to shoot. But now it was difficult to find the arrows in the grass. Unlike Bunzo's, they didn't fall very close together.

He cleaned the tips of the arrows and released the string from the bow before putting them away. Walking back to the judge's house, he felt strange. Even though he had used the bow all day, he did not feel relieved at setting it aside. Instead, he felt as if a part of himself was missing.

The judge was away on business. Normally he went to investigate reports of wrongdoing in the surrounding district. A few days ago, however, he had been called to Edo. The summons was impossible to refuse, for it came from the shogun, the military commander who ruled Japan.

Seikei had met the shogun once, on the occasion when the judge asked permission to adopt him. The shogun had been courteous, even friendly. Although, of course, he had been the host of a tea ceremony, and thus was required to treat everyone present as a friend—even if he were a lowly merchant's son.

Tonight, the judge's housekeeper, Noka, had prepared trays of food for everyone in the household. Bunzo and the three other samurai guards were already eating. Seikei sat cross-legged on the floor with the others, balancing his bamboo tray on his knees.

Noka, like Bunzo, disapproved of Seikei, but she apparently felt that the best way to turn him into a samurai was to feed him as much as he could eat. On his tray rested a bowl of *miso* soup made from soybeans, two kinds of rice, several small dishes of pickled vegetables, morsels of roasted tofu, and—most special of all—a covered bamboo container of steamed fish. Looking at the food, Seikei could well understand why the judge himself was fat.

As Seikei picked up his chopsticks, he glanced at a small shrine in a corner of the room. It contained a scroll painting of the first Tokugawa shogun, Ieyasu. The judge put it there as a sign of respect and honor for the Tokugawa family. But Seikei couldn't help noticing that Ieyasu was an even fatter man than the judge himself. Perhaps that was why his portrait looked down on the table where the judge ate.

Bunzo suddenly looked up. Though he had hardly moved, the other three guards reached for their swords, which they had set beside them while eating. Only then did Seikei hear what Bunzo had: the sound of hoofbeats approaching outside.

"Only one rider," said Bunzo. "A messenger." The others nodded and picked up their chopsticks again. In a moment, Noka slid open the door and entered. Kneeling before Bunzo, she presented a lacquered letter box with Judge Ooka's crest on it.

Bunzo opened it, took out a piece of paper, and unfolded it. Seikei recognized the judge's brush-stroke writing. Bunzo read the message silently, and then repeated it aloud: "The Flowers of Edo are blooming. Come at once with everyone available."

The others rose and left the room. Bunzo stood and said to Seikei, "Can you ride fast enough to keep up with us?"

"I'll try," Seikei replied. He had made progress in riding a horse and now could stay on even at a gallop. "But . . . what does the message mean? Are we going to ride at night to view flowers? What kind?"

"It's an old Edo saying," Bunzo told him. "It means that the city is on fire."

2

THE SILK SELLER'S STORY

The people of Edo feared fires more than the threat of any approaching army of samurai. For fire came without warning, often while the city slept, and spread more swiftly than warriors on horseback. Edo was crowded, and many of its houses had been built in haste. They were flimsy, made of light wood with paper windows. Once a flame got out of control, it licked down the packed rows of houses in the blink of an eye.

This was true in all the cities of Japan. Seikei remembered how often his father in Osaka had warned everyone in the shop to be careful of lamps and candles. Even at night, when everything but the kitchen fire was extinguished, Seikei could hear his father rise from his sleeping mat, padding softly through the rooms and sniffing loudly for traces of smoke.

When Seikei was five years old, another part of Osaka had burned. He remembered the foul-smelling haze that hung over the city for days. He had caught a glimpse of someone who had been horribly burned being carried into a house near theirs. Seikei thought at first that the man's clothes had burned and hung loosely around him. But then he saw that the blackened, peeling strips were the man's own skin.

The memory kept him awake as he rode through the night with Bunzo and the other three samurai. They had left as soon as they saddled the horses, taking nothing with them except the clothes they wore and their swords. Seikei did not as yet carry the two swords—one short, one long—that samurai alone were entitled to wear. Because he had not finished his training, he still used the plain wooden sword the judge had given him earlier. He slipped it inside his *obi,* or belt, above the three-quarter length trousers that samurai wore. As Seikei mounted his horse, the sword lifted up the back of his travel jacket, which had the judge's crest embroidered on it.

Normally, Edo was almost a day's ride from the judge's house in the countryside. But because there were no people walking on the Tokaido Road at night, Seikei and the others could ride much faster. The rapid pace kept Seikei alert. He had to concentrate all his efforts to remaining seated on the horse. He knew that if he fell, he would have to pick himself off the ground and catch his horse by himself. For the others would not stop for such a trivial reason when they were answering a summons from their lord.

Seikei had no idea how close they were to Edo until he smelled the smoke. He raised his head and looked into the eastern sky. The moon had set some time before, and he spied what he thought was the first glimmer of sunrise. Then he saw the tongues of red orange light flicker, and knew that they must be the flames of burning houses.

The horses were well trained, but even so, they shied away from the smoke. Finally, the riders had to dismount and lead them forward by the reins. At the guardhouse at the Nihombashi Bridge, Seikei and the others left the horses behind.

Even on foot, it was difficult to cross the bridge. They had to fight their way against a stream of people who were headed in the opposite direction. They were Edokkai, citizens of Edo, trying to flee. Many carried possessions on their backs or had crying children in their arms.

Bunzo cried out, "Make way! Make way!" Yet the fear of being engulfed by flames was greater than the respect that normally would have made people obey a samurai's command. If Bunzo had wished, he could have drawn his sword and hacked his way mercilessly through the crowd. But the judge frowned on such methods.

Finally, they reached the other side of the bridge. Bunzo led them through darkened streets, somehow avoiding the main thoroughfares that were choked with people. It was not long before they came in sight of the fire itself. They came closer, feeling the heat intensify, until finally they stood in the street where it burned most ferociously.

Seikei stood and watched, fascinated. The flames had already left behind many blocks of charred ruins, the remnants of houses and stores. Here, they were licking greedily at another row of buildings, sending sparks and fiery brands high into the air. At any moment, it seemed, the fire might leap across the street where Seikei stood.

But an army of silent figures worked furiously to stop it. Dressed in leather coats and helmets, three lines of men sent buckets of water from hand to hand. Those at the end of the line—heroes! thought Seikei—climbed ladders to douse the roofs nearest the flames with water. Each time the fire tried to advance, it gave an angry hiss as the water turned to steam.

Down the street, a smaller group of men, wearing uniforms emblazoned with a crest identifying them as part of the fire squad, were throwing ropes with heavy metal hooks onto roofs. Their purpose, Seikei knew, was to pull down the houses before the flames could reach them. Without fuel, the fire might burn itself out.

Seikei realized he was not the only one watching the fire. Others, perhaps people who had lived in the burned area, had gathered. Seikei understood why. Though the fire destroyed everything in its path, it had awesome power and beauty. The kami of the fire must be a terrible spirit like Susanoo, the uncontrollable brother of the sun goddess Amaterasu. Susanoo was feared, but he was also worshiped because of his great power.

Seikei saw the orange light from the fire flicker across the faces of the watching crowd. It made them seem as if they too were on fire. He saw that some were weeping. No doubt they had lost their homes and possessions and had nowhere to go.

But as the fire caught a straw roof and blazed upward, Seikei had a sudden glimpse of a very different face. It had a look of joy, even of triumph. Seikei was so surprised that he took a step forward to see it better.

Just then, however, a bucket of water drove the flames back momentarily. Steam and smoke clouded the air, and when they dissipated, the face was gone.

Seikei had no time to pursue it, for another figure—a more familiar one—appeared. It was a man as wide as two ordinary men, taller than average too. He walked as slowly and calmly as if he were alone in a pine forest.

It could be no one else but Seikei's patron and foster father, Judge Ooka. Bunzo had been more alert than Seikei and was already at his side, nodding as the judge spoke.

Seikei hurried to catch up. By the time he reached the judge, Bunzo had already received his instructions and was off to carry them out.

The judge acknowledged Seikei's greeting with a nod. "I am ready to help," Seikei said.

"Yes," the judge replied. "Every person must join in the effort. Let me see your hands."

Surprised, Seikei held them out, palms up. "I see that you have been practicing kyudo," the judge said. "Are you making progress?"

Seikei bowed his head. "Not very much," he admitted.

"You are thinking too hard about it," the judge said.

"Bunzo has told me the same," Seikei replied. "But I do not understand. Why is it not good to concentrate on improvement?"

"A good question," said the judge. "The answer is difficult. It is because the mind wants to control the body. To achieve mastery, the body must learn to move *without* thought. The act of shooting an arrow—or indeed, any act that requires skill—must be as natural as pulling one's hand from a fire. A true master achieves the level of nonthinking called *muga*, in which the mind does not interfere with the body."

"Bunzo instructed me to shoot arrows without a target."

"That is a good start," said the judge. "But there are other problems that require our attention now. This fire, for example. The shogun has entrusted me with the task of preventing fires in the city. Some years ago, I recommended that each district in the city have its own fire squad. Towers were built where lookouts could sound an alarm at the first sign of fire. That system has worked well, until this latest outbreak."

Seikei remembered that the shogun had summoned Judge Ooka to his court in Edo ten days earlier. "Has the fire been going on that long?" Seikei asked.

"This is the third fire that has broken out since I arrived," the judge told him. "There were two others the week before."

"Aii," replied Seikei. "What is causing them?"

The judge nodded. "The first question. Some fires cannot be avoided. Lightning may strike if the kami have been offended or are merely playful. Someone may be careless with a lantern from time to time. But for five fires to occur in such a brief span . . . someone must be causing them."

"But who would do such a horrible thing?" asked Seikei.

The judge looked upward, where men carrying buckets ran across a tiled roof. Their *geta*, wooden shoes, made a clattering noise on the ceramic tiles. "The proper question, I think, is why," he said. "When we discover why, we may know who."

From above them came the sound of a mighty hiss and suddenly the street became dark. A few small flames still flickered behind windows down the street. But already the fire squads were climbing the walls with ladders to extinguish them.

"For now," the judge said, "it seems that the fire has been conquered. But the firefighters are exhausted. So many fires within a short time has put great demands on them. Many people have been forced to flee. I fear that if this continues, the city will be consumed. And since the shogun has entrusted me with its safety, I will bear the disgrace."

That frightened Seikei more than anything else he had heard or seen that night. The thought of the judge being disgraced was unbearable.

The judge began to walk toward the area that had been burned down. Seikei followed. Little remained of the buildings themselves, but in the ashes, Seikei saw things that had been only partially burned. Many seemed to be looms, the frames that were used to make cloth.

In Edo, artisans and merchants of different kinds lived and worked in their own sections of the city. Seikei guessed that this must have been the neighborhood where one could go to purchase silk, linen, or other kinds of cloth.

The judge said, "Use your sharp eyes. If you see something that is out of the ordinary, tell me."

Then Seikei remembered. "I have already seen something," he said. He told the judge about the face he had seen in the crowd—the one that seemed to take joy from the fire's destruction.

The judge nodded. "Bunzo has gone to find people who had shops in the area. The lookout for this district was able to see where the fire broke out. I want you to study the faces of the people Bunzo brings to us. Signal me if you think any of them was the one you saw."

They went to a small house on the edge of the burned district. It was the home of the watchtower guard. When the judge entered, the guard knelt and touched his forehead on the floor. "I am ashamed," he said. "It was my carelessness that has caused all this."

"Not at all," replied the judge. "Rise and take comfort in the thought that your quick action saved the fire from being worse than it was."

The guard's wife brought tea for the judge and Seikei. She shuffled across the floor on her knees, both entering and leaving the room. Seikei knew that the judge disliked such displays of respect, but as the shogun's high official, he couldn't avoid them.

Not long afterward, Bunzo arrived, bringing five women with him. As soon as they entered the room, they prostrated themselves on the floor, no doubt because Bunzo told them of the judge's rank.

"Sit up!" the judge called, in the voice he used when he wanted to be obeyed at once. "Let me see your faces."

Seikei knew that this was for his benefit. He carefully studied the upraised faces. It was hard to tell, because he had glimpsed the one in the crowd only for a second. None of these were showing any signs of happiness or triumph. Fear, mostly, and a great deal of sadness, for of course these people must have lost every-thing in the fire. Their clothes were smudged with soot. Seikei could see that their hands and arms were burned, no doubt in the struggle to salvage something from the flames.

The judge glanced at Seikei, who shook his head slightly. None of the prisoners resembled the woman he'd seen.

The judge turned his attention back to the prisoners. "Does anyone wish to confess to setting the fire?" he asked.

They stirred uneasily, avoiding his eyes. The judge usually began his examinations this way. "Since I will learn the truth eventually," he had once told Seikei, "wouldn't it be easier if the criminal told me at once?"

Seikei had yet to see that happen, but this time he was surprised. A woman in the second row spoke up. She was wearing an ordinary blue cotton kimono, but Seikei noticed the obi around her waist was of high-quality silk. "I did not set the fire, Lord, but it began in my shop."

The judge gave an approving nod. "Come closer and tell me what you know," he said.

Drawing her kimono around her, she shuffled on her knees to the front of the room, where the judge sat cross-legged on a mat. "A woman came to my shop looking for silk to make a kimono," she said. "She was a *geisha*."

"What led you to think that?" the judge asked.

The woman seemed surprised. "Why . . . she had her hair arranged in the fashion of a geisha. Her eyebrows were shaved. And she wore a silk kimono so costly that no one but a geisha could afford it."

"Describe the kimono," said the judge.

She thought. "It was brown, reddish brown like the color of maple leaves that have fallen. Cranes were embroidered on it with gold thread. I knew it cost a lot. I figured she might be a good customer."

Judge Ooka nodded. "Very well. She came to your shop for silk. What happened?"

"I showed her several kinds, but she wasn't satisfied." The memory of it seemed to annoy the woman even now. Her forehead creased. "I have the very *best* silk," she said. "None better in Edo. My daughters gather the silk cocoons and unwind them—"

The judge raised his hand. "I will accept that your silk is the finest in Edo. Why was the woman dissatisfied with it?"

"She gave no reason. These geishas, some of them are as arrogant as if they were married to a daimyo."

"So she left?"

"No. I wish that she had. For some reason, I was determined to please her. I went to a storeroom to find some more samples of silk. While I was gone, she set fire to the store!"

Judge Ooka nodded as if the woman had said something quite ordinary. "Of course," he pointed out mildly, "you did not see her do that."

"What else could have happened?" the woman argued. "When I returned, the paper windows were aflame. So were the mats in the front room. She must have emptied the oil lamp onto them. It was a vicious, vicious act."

"It certainly was," agreed the judge, "if it happened that way. But what if the lamp overturned by accident and she fled to avoid being burned?"

"Then why not call out?" the woman asked. "Why did she not sound an alarm? I might have been able to put the fire out if I had discovered it sooner. No, she did it deliberately."

The judge thought about this. "And so you have no place to stay, now that your shop has been destroyed?" he asked.

"I have nothing," the woman said. It was as if she had just realized this.

"Bunzo, make sure she has a safe place to stay," said the judge.

"Oh," said the woman. "I can stay with my daughters in the country."

"It would be too difficult a journey right now," said the judge. "And I may think of some more questions to ask you."

The woman looked unhappier than ever as Bunzo led her away. After a few more questions, Judge Ooka dismissed the other prisoners. When they were gone, he sipped the tea.

"Why would a geisha set fire to a silk merchant's shop?" the judge asked.

Seikei wasn't sure if he really wanted an answer. "Perhaps she didn't," Seikei suggested.

The judge nodded. "Tomorrow we will search for the geisha," he said.

3

DEATH IN A TEAHOUSE

*S*eikei rose at dawn. He had trained himself by now to waken when the first sunlight crept across the mat where he slept. He sat on the floor and meditated, trying to clear his mind of distractions. But thoughts from last night kept intruding.

Was the woman telling the truth? That was one question the judge had not asked. It was the duty of a judge to obtain a confession. That was proof that the criminal had been discovered. If the judge wished, he could have any suspected person tortured to obtain a confession.

Judge Ooka, however, disapproved of torture. Not because he was tenderhearted. But as he told Seikei, "Many people will confess to anything to avoid being tortured. This is obvious. Therefore, torture may result in the wrong person being punished while the real criminal goes free. It is my duty to preserve order by discovering criminals—not merely to frighten someone into confessing."

The judge usually listened to people's answers and

tried to find, as he said, the correct path to the criminal. It didn't seem to bother him that sometimes people lied to him.

Sighing, Seikei stood up from his meditation. He had, once more, failed to achieve the concentration he wanted.

After a breakfast of rice and melon, he and the judge set out on foot. The smell of smoke still hung in the air. "Where is Bunzo?" Seikei asked.

"He has many other duties," replied the judge. "If someone is deliberately setting fires, then the fire lookouts must increase their vigilance. Bunzo knows how to organize such efforts."

They walked in a circular path toward the eastern edge of the city. It was impossible to travel in a straight line from one part of Edo to another. A series of moats, connected to the city's two rivers, formed a spiral around the shogun's castle. The intricate waterways made the city's heart easier to defend, for nowhere could a hostile force attack it head-on. The only drawback was that it made everyday traveling difficult too.

Seikei and the judge reached the Sumida River, where a few small boats were moored. A couple of boatmen, clad in loincloths, waved and called out. They were pleased at the prospect of customers so early in the day. The judge chose a boat that looked sufficiently sturdy, and stepped aboard. "Take us to Yoshiwara," he said.

The man nodded, but said, "My lord, they will be asleep there now."

"They will wake for me," said the judge.

The man gave him a second look and seemed to recognize him. He gave a deep bow and waited until they were seated before pushing the boat offshore. The boat glided silently away from the dock, propelled by the long pole the boatman held. Mist was rising from the water. Up ahead lay the region of marshes where "the floating world" was.

Seikei felt a tingle of excitement as they approached. His father—his old father, the merchant—had always warned him never to set foot in the floating world. It was called that not because it was built on water, but because it was a place where dreams were the only things that were real. People went there for relief from their everyday lives. They could attend *kabuki* theaters, enjoying the music, color, and dance. But most visitors to the floating world went there to be entertained by geishas— the women who spent their lives learning to please men. Geishas practiced the arts of music, dancing, song, and conversation, all to make men forget their cares.

Going upriver, the trip was short and soon the boatman tucked his craft alongside the quay at Yoshiwara. Seikei and the judge disembarked, and the judge handed the boatman a coin. A few steps away, they hailed the gatekeeper, who lowered a drawbridge to let them cross the river.

When they reached the other side, the gatekeeper eyed their swords. "You must leave those here," he said.

To Seikei's surprise, the judge removed the two swords from his obi and placed them in a wooden case in the gatehouse. Seikei did the same with his polished wooden sword.

As they walked off, Seikei asked the judge why he had agreed to give up what were a samurai's most prized possessions. "The gatekeeper was only doing his duty," said the judge. "It is the shogun's order that all swords must be left here. Formerly, there were many fights among those who visited Yoshiwara. Without swords, they are less likely to do serious injury to one another."

"But you are the shogun's official," said Seikei. "You have a good reason for carrying your swords here."

"I do not think I will have to defend myself," said the judge. "Besides, I would not set a very good example if I disobeyed the law. If those entrusted with carrying out the laws ignore them, then why should anyone obey them?"

Seikei saw the truth of this. In any case, he had yet to see the judge draw his sword from the scabbard for any reason. Seikei doubted he would need to do it here, where most of the residents seemed to be asleep. Near the gate, only one shop had an open door. The blue banner displayed above it read: Hats and Clothing for Rent.

Seikei pointed it out to the judge. "Why would any-one come here to rent clothing?" he asked.

"Because they do not wish to be recognized," the judge replied. "Some daimyos and officials enjoy the pleasures of the teahouses, but do not wish their pres-ence to become known. In any case, the first-rank geishas—the *tayu*—are not awed by a man's rank in so-ciety."

"Not even yours?" asked Seikei.

"A tayu," said the judge, "may accept or turn down anyone she wishes. She may even choose a wealthy mer-chant over a daimyo."

Seikei was astonished. The thought that his first fa-ther, the merchant, might be favored over a daimyo, a samurai lord, was impossible to comprehend. "If that is true, then Yoshiwara is indeed a different world," he told the judge.

"We shall see. For now, let us observe." They turned a corner and entered one of Yoshiwara's main streets. The houses here were decorated with bright banners. Pretty paper lanterns, unlit at this time of day, hung from the doorways and the branches of the cherry trees that lined the street. Seikei could easily imagine how dazzling the scene must look at night.

Then he noticed something else, something strange. He walked over to the doorstep of one of the teahouses. Someone had poured a trail of white dust around the steps. Not only here, but in front of many of the tea-houses along the street.

Seikei picked up a few grains of the white dust and tasted it. "Salt," he said.

The judge stood beside him, nodding. "People commonly put salt at the entrances to their houses when they fear a demon will try to enter."

Seikei nodded. They did that in Osaka too. "Do you think demons exist?" he asked the judge.

"I have not seen one," said the judge. "But then perhaps that is because I have been fooled."

Seikei smiled. He doubted that anyone could fool the judge. "How could that happen?"

"I may have seen demons who disguised themselves as men," the judge replied. He pointed to one of the teahouses. Attached to its front porch was a mourning notice—a white paper in a black frame that told of the death of one of the occupants. "Let us investigate there," said the judge.

Seikei followed—reluctantly, for he had little experience with the dead, except for the benign ancestral spirits that returned to earth at the Bon Festival. At the top of the steps the judge pulled a cord that hung in front of the door. Seikei could hear a bell clang overhead. In a moment a small girl, about ten, slid the door open a crack and peered out. "I am very sorry," she said. "We are closed. Please do not ring the bell."

"I am Judge Ooka, the shogun's official," the judge

told her. "I must speak to the proprietor of this house at once."

The girl's eyes opened wide. She looked nervously behind her. "It would be better to come back later," she said.

"I have no time," the judge responded.

The girl nodded. "Please wait," she said, turning and shutting the door. Soon it slid open again, revealing an older woman with sharp, calculating eyes. She gestured for the judge and Seikei to come inside.

They stood in a hallway with doors leading off in three directions. A small shrine to a Buddhist saint stood in a corner. A candle flickered in front of it. That usually meant someone in the household had died recently. Seikei could hear the soft tones of a gong coming from elsewhere in the house. That too signaled the presence of a dead person.

The older woman bowed before the judge. "I regret," she said, "that I cannot invite you further inside. We are having a vigil. The priest is here."

"Who has died?" asked the judge.

"One of my employees," said the woman. "A girl named Akiko. She had no family, so . . ." She shrugged. "I paid for the priest and for a cremation. That was foolish, but I have a big heart."

Seikei thought this unlikely, but then rebuked himself. The judge had told him not to come to hasty conclusions.

"What did she die of?" asked the judge.

The woman lowered her eyes. "She drowned herself in the canal."

"I would like to see her," said the judge.

The request agitated the woman. "You will have to undergo purification afterward," she protested. "I cannot be responsible. I am not at fault."

"Show me," the judge said firmly.

The woman shrugged and slid open another door. From where he stood, Seikei could see a large tub-shaped coffin with the lid closed. Candles were set around it. A Buddhist monk in an orange robe sat cross-legged on the floor, ringing a small gong and chanting prayers.

Without going into the room, the judge nodded. Relieved, the woman closed the door again. "Has one of the shogun's officials seen the body?" the judge asked.

"Why . . . no," the woman admitted. "But I reported it. As soon as the *hinin* brought her here." Hinin were outcasts who would do loathsome tasks such as touching dead bodies. "It's them you should be accusing. I'm sure they stole the kimono she was wearing."

"What kind of kimono was it?" the judge asked. The woman did not notice the change in his voice, but Seikei did.

The woman furrowed her brow. "It was like the color of autumn leaves—red with a touch of brown. Beautiful embroidery, in real gold thread. It had a crane design.

Very elegant. You would think if Akiko were going to kill herself, she might have . . ."

She trailed off without finishing the sentence, but Seikei knew what she was thinking. Why wear your best kimono if you're going to drown yourself? Leave it for someone else to wear.

The judge asked, "How did she come to have such a fine kimono? Do you pay your employees that well?"

The woman gave him a sidelong look, wondering if he were accusing her of being stingy. "Well enough," she replied. "But that kimono was given to her by a geisha, one of the best. Umae herself."

The judge nodded. "Why such an expensive gift?"

The woman shrugged. "Akiko saved Umae from an embarrassing situation. Umae was entertaining guests here, when another party of men arrived. Akiko recognized one of them as Umae's special friend—at least *he* thought he was—and warned her. Then Akiko managed to get the special friend off to our second-best room, and he never knew Umae was here at all."

The judge nodded. "She must have been a resourceful person."

The woman smiled, exposing teeth that she had deliberately blackened, as was the fashion. "Oh yes, I would say so. Not going to be easy to replace."

"Then why would she kill herself?" asked the judge.

"Who knows? She was from the countryside. Perhaps she had grand dreams and one day realized they would never come true. That happens to everyone here in Yoshiwara. Some take it better than others."

The judge nodded. "Yes, people have different ways of dealing with disappointment." He paused and then changed the subject. "And you say you reported her death? When was this?"

"Yesterday morning. Some fishermen saw her body floating and called for the hinin. Someone recognized her hairpins, and they brought her here. I sent someone to the magistrate to report the death. It is required."

"But no official examined her body?"

"No, but they wouldn't need to. She was dead, all right." She gave another black-toothed smile.

"Take the lid off the coffin," said the judge. "I will examine her."

The woman opened her mouth, horrified. She started to protest, but the judge had already slid open the door and entered the room. Seikei was obliged to follow, though he shared the woman's fears. Death was the most unclean of all life's stages. Coming close to it required anyone but a hinin to undergo a cleansing ritual afterward.

The judge bowed politely to the Buddhist monk, who showed no surprise at seeing him again. Nor did he betray any emotion—except possibly to chant a little louder—when the woman shook her head and lifted the lid of the coffin. The carpenter had not yet arrived to nail it shut.

Seikei hung back, but the judge motioned him to come closer. Inside the coffin, as was customary, the woman was seated in the lotus position, Buddha-like. She was clothed in a white shroud that hid even her face. On her lap lay a knife. That too was a custom, to allow the dead person to defend herself against demons who might block her path to the next life. But this knife seemed larger and more dangerous than others Seikei had seen. And the dead woman's hand had been wrapped around it.

His attention was drawn elsewhere as the judge reached out and gently moved the top of the shroud. Seikei wanted to stop him, but fortunately managed to control himself.

He tried to look away, but then he caught a glimpse of the young woman's face. She had been pretty, though not as beautiful as a geisha. But now, in death, her head had been shaved. She showed signs that she had struggled to avoid her fate. Her face looked angry.

The judge adjusted the cloth to its original position and then, with Seikei's help, replaced the cover on the coffin. As he turned, he handed the monk a coin. "Pray awhile longer," said the judge. "She is not yet at peace."

4

THE FORTUNE-TELLER'S PREDICTION

After they left the teahouse, the judge and Seikei looked for a place to bathe. It was necessary to purify themselves after being in the presence of death. They spotted a blue banner advertising a bathhouse and went inside. After the judge paid the attendant, the two of them were soon soaking in a pool of hot water.

The judge seemed in no hurry. Seikei knew that one of the places he enjoyed most was the bath in his country house west of Edo. There, of course, the water was warmer because the judge had built a system of bamboo pipes to bring water from nearby hot springs.

Seikei was restless, however. He must have shown it, for the judge asked him, "What conclusions have you drawn?"

Seikei thought carefully. "I have concluded that the dead girl's kimono sounds like the one worn by the geisha who started the fire."

"I think you have gone farther than I," said the judge.

Seikei hung his head. That meant he had gone too far.

"We still do not know the geisha started the fire," said the judge. "Although it seems likely. Perhaps it was *this* young woman who started the fire. She may have looked like a geisha to the owner of the cloth shop. Working in a teahouse, she might have wanted to be a geisha, and would have known how to make herself up as one."

"And then she drowned herself? But what happened to her kimono?" asked Seikei.

"It could be as her employer thinks—someone stole it from her after her body was found," replied the judge.

"Maybe it was stolen *before* she died," suggested Seikei.

"Why would you think that?" asked the judge.

"Because . . . because she looked as if she had struggled. Not as if she drowned herself on purpose."

"You observe well," said the judge.

Seikei's face flushed with pride to hear that.

"One other thing," the judge said. "Did you notice it?"

"The knife?" asked Seikei.

The judge nodded. "Someone thinks that the demon is quite real. That will make the case more difficult to solve."

Seikei couldn't see why. "Because a demon is more dangerous?" he asked.

"No," said the judge. "Because it means people will be more afraid." He sighed. "I suppose we have purified ourselves enough. No one has come by to add hot water to the bath."

After toweling off and dressing, they went into the street again. It seemed as deserted as ever, even though the sun was nearly at its highest point. They stopped at several more teahouses, but learned nothing. At each one, the people inside seemed reluctant to answer questions. The judge's presence only made them more nervous. When he asked about the drowned girl, everyone denied knowing her.

"I didn't know the others, either," said a woman at the fifth teahouse they visited.

The judge paused. "Which others?" he asked.

The woman looked away. "Well, the others you were asking about."

"I mentioned no one else. Who were you thinking of?"

She shrugged. "Other women—two of them. People talk. Idle gossip. I know nothing about them. Forgive me, Lord."

The judge paused, then pressed on. "You say there were two others? Don't you mean three?"

She gave him a startled look. "No," she said. "I heard of two only, before this one."

Much to Seikei's surprise, the judge stood and thanked the woman for her cooperation. Seikei saw the look of relief on her face as the judge turned to leave.

Outside, Seikei must have shown his own puzzlement, for the judge said, "Do you think the woman knew more than she told us?"

"Why . . . of course," Seikei replied.

"She was afraid," said the judge. "Clearly the woman whose body we saw today was not the first death. Now it is obvious why all these teahouses have salt in front of them."

"But why didn't you make her tell you more?"

"A person who is afraid is difficult to question. She might make up some tale just to satisfy me. We can find another person who will give us better information." The judge pointed to a banner on a shop farther down the street. It was a fortune-teller's. "Should we have our fortunes told?" he asked.

Perhaps the judge was testing him, Seikei thought. He tried to come up with the right answer. "It would be better not to be distracted from our path," he said. Once before, the judge had sent Seikei to investigate a crime. The judge's only instruction had been to "follow the path."

The judge smiled. "That is true, but I wish to see the path more clearly before proceeding."

"Do you think the fortune-teller will know where the criminal will strike next?"

"Probably not," the judge replied. "I do not think anyone can see into the future. That would require one to know not only what men do, but what the kami intend. For example, I can tell you that we will return to my house in Edo tonight. That seems certain to me. But if a storm arises and our boat cannot make the journey, we shall have to find lodging elsewhere. Or I may receive information that will require you to stay here."

"Me?" Seikei didn't like the sound his voice made. It showed he was caught off guard. So he added hastily, "Of course I am ready to do whatever you wish."

"I was only using that as an example," said the judge. "As you see, the possibilities are endless."

"Yet many people do believe in fortune-tellers," Seikei suggested. He was thinking of his father—the merchant—who consulted several different fortune-tellers before he made any important business decision.

"As do I," said the judge. Seikei sighed, for as the judge often did, he was taking both sides of an argument.

The judge sought to enlighten him. "A fortune-teller, to be successful, must do the same thing that I do."

"What is that?" Seikei asked.

"Observe people closely," replied the judge.

The fortune-teller was a woman whose age it was impossible to guess. She wore a black wig and the white face makeup of a geisha, with eyebrows shaved and redrawn high on her forehead. Her dark eyes flicked over Seikei and the judge as they entered. She was seated on the floor behind a low table that was set with cups of different-colored liquids. Behind her on the wall was a print of a particularly fearsome-looking dragon with red eyes. The air in the room was perfumed with a heavy incense from sticks that were burning slowly in a bowl of sand.

The judge made an admiring comment about the bowl. The woman was pleased and protested that it was only a worthless object. "The Judge Ooka, about whom everyone speaks, must have much better pieces than this at his estate," she said. Seikei was startled, wondering how she had recognized the judge.

The woman tapped a small gong with her fingernail and almost at once a girl entered the room. She carried a large pillow covered with green silk. After she placed it on the floor, the fortune-teller motioned to the judge to sit. The girl disappeared, having left no pillow for Seikei. He knelt and rested on the back of his heels. The ordinary position was comfortable enough for him.

"Since you know who I am," said the judge, "you must know what questions I want to ask."

The woman smiled. "Everyone knows you have come because of the demon who has killed three girls in Yoshiwara."

Seikei was surprised, but tried not to show it. That

was not, of course, the reason why the judge had come to Yoshiwara. However, it was part of his method to allow people to lead him to the solution to a problem.

"Then why are people reluctant to help me?" the judge asked.

The woman spread her hands. "They do not know who is more powerful, you or the demon. So they try not to offend either of you."

"Is that why no one reported these crimes to the local magistrate?"

"Oh, he knows of them," she said. "But he is not like you."

"In what way?"

"He would gladly punish anyone who disobeyed the shogun's laws—as long as it was someone from Yoshiwara. But since it is a demon, he too fears to act. You, however, have no fear. You will pursue injustice and evil wherever they lead."

"Do not flatter me," said the judge. "You might cloud my judgment."

"As you wish," the woman said. Her hand fluttered like a butterfly landing on a flower.

"What form does this demon take?" asked the judge.

"If he comes from outside, he must be a customer," replied the woman. "A man who seeks enjoyment here—relaxation, relief from care, freedom from duty."

"That does not help me," said the judge. "Who were these girls seen with?"

"Two of them were tayu, geishas of the highest class," the fortune-teller said. "They were not obliged to take customers they did not want. Therefore, they were most often in the company of daimyos, high officials of the shogun's government, or wealthy merchants." She fluttered her hands. "You see how it is?"

"I understand," said the judge. "But what of the most recent girl? She was no geisha."

The woman nodded. "Only a teahouse attendant. But the two geishas who died—they often met their customers at that same teahouse. It was a very fashionable place, very elegant. Many of the best customers used to go there."

"No longer?" asked the judge.

The woman raised her eyes to the ceiling. "If you wished to have a good time, enjoy yourself, forget your worries . . ."

"I would not go to where a person has recently died," the judge finished.

She nodded.

"Where will the most fashionable geishas go to meet their customers now?" he asked.

"You ask me to see into the future," said the woman. "For that I must concentrate."

The judge reached into his sleeve and took out a cloth pouch. From this he drew a few silver *mon* and put them on the table.

The woman hardly glanced at them. She sighed and

said, "I will do my best." From underneath the table she brought a wooden box that had on its side the *yin-yang* symbol—a circle divided in two by a wavy line. One side of the circle was of dark wood; the other was light.

Seikei had seen this kind of fortune-teller once before when his father the merchant took him to one in Osaka. On that occasion the fortune-teller said that Seikei would become a rich and powerful merchant. He hoped this fortune would be more accurate.

The woman took a handful of yarrow sticks from the box and abruptly threw them on the table. She studied the forms they made and said, "The Teahouse of the Falling Cherry Blossoms will be the most favored one," she said. "Oba Koko, the owner, has persuaded the geisha Umae to host her parties there." Then she poked one of the sticks with her fingernail. "However," she added, "great danger awaits for the unwary."

Seikei was sure that would be the next place they would go. But once they were outside, the judge surprised him again. "I must go visit the local magistrate," he said. "It would be better if you did not accompany me."

Seikei must have shown his disappointment, for the judge said, "Sometimes it is necessary for me to correct others. I fear the local magistrate has neglected his duty by not investigating the deaths of the two geishas. It would be embarrassing for him if you were present during our conversation."

Seikei was relieved. "Should I wait for you at the dock?"

"No," said the judge. "I thought you heard what the fortune-teller said."

Seikei blinked. "Yes, I did."

"Then you recalled the possibility I mentioned earlier."

"You mean . . . that I would stay here?" Seikei's stomach felt as if it were suddenly empty.

"Now we know," said the judge, "where the path should take you."

5

SEIKEI THE THIEF

When Seikei arrived, a woman in a plum-colored kimono was just chasing a boy out the door with a broomstick. That was fortunate for Seikei, even though he did not yet know it. The boy kept ducking his head and dodging, but the woman's blows kept raining down on him, forcing him down the steps of the front porch. At last, the boy escaped by running down the street.

The woman stood on the steps, rearranging her kimono, which had become a little undone. She caught sight of Seikei watching her.

"What do you want?" she asked crossly. "I'm busy right now. The teahouse is closed."

Seikei could see by the banner hanging from the second floor that he had reached the right place. This was the Teahouse of the Falling Cherry Blossoms. He hoped, however, that he had the wrong person.

"Are you the owner of this teahouse?" he asked.

She looked at him suspiciously. "Why do you ask?

Have I done something wrong? I am but a humble person, trying to make a living in a harsh world."

Seikei thought to himself that she acted as if there were no one of higher rank in all Yoshiwara, much less in the teahouse. He bowed respectfully and said, "I am looking for work and would like to see the owner."

She looked him over closely. "You don't appear to have done much work. You're not a farmer, because your hands are clean. You're not a samurai—not arrogant enough. Even though your hair is cut like a samurai's, you don't fool Oba Koko. Nor an artisan because then you would have learned a skill and wouldn't seek work here. So you must be a merchant's son, accustomed to luxury and idleness."

Seikei cringed. Even becoming the adopted son of a samurai had not changed him. People still knew, just by looking, who his real father had been. Perhaps it was as Bunzo had once said: "A fish cannot learn to sing, even if you put him in a cage."

None of that mattered, he told himself. He must obey the judge's command. He bowed again. "You have keen sight," he said. "But I assure you I am willing to work hard."

"Hmp," she sniffed. "Perhaps you are a demon then. You don't look like one, but then who can be sure?" All at once, she reached out and pinched his nose. Hard.

He cried out and pulled away from her. Oba Koko

nodded with satisfaction. "That's settled then. A demon will never let you pinch his nose." She looked at him again. "Are you ready to clean the floor when some drunken daimyo has been sick?"

"Yes," he said, trying not to think how that would be.

"What if a samurai becomes rough and frightens the geisha? What would you do?"

Seikei thought. "Um . . . ask him to leave?"

She cackled. "No! You sneak up behind and hit him with a club." She slammed the end of her broomstick onto the porch railing to demonstrate. "Then toss him in the street. Can you do that? Or are you afraid?"

"But . . . a samurai may kill anyone who displeases him."

"Why do you think they have to leave their swords at the entrance to Yoshiwara? Because here in the floating world, the rules are different." Abruptly, she handed him the broomstick. "Here," she said. "You are lucky I lost my patience with that worthless nephew of mine, Kiru. I need to hire someone before tonight, and here you are. It may be an omen, who knows? I am Oba Koko. From now on obey me without question and you may stay here." She made it sound like a great privilege.

Seikei followed her into the house, thinking that Oba Koko would be a harsher master than the judge.

He wasn't wrong.

Oba Koko led him straight through the house to the kitchen at the rear. A heavy-looking woman with silver strands in her hair was examining some fresh carp that lay on a table. Next to her were three empty jars, a large pot of rice, and a jug of vinegar. Seikei had seen his mother in Osaka combine these ingredients to preserve fish that would be served later.

"We have a new nephew," Oba Koko told the woman. She turned to Seikei. "This is Ryori. You will obey her without question as well."

"My name is Seikei," he said quietly.

Oba Koko waved that away. "We will call you nephew. Giving people names only confuses things and gives them ideas."

Seikei wasn't sure which ideas she meant, but he held his tongue. Just then a girl staggered into the room, carrying a heavy wooden bucket of water with both hands. Some of the water splashed onto the floor.

"Look at this, Tsune," Oba Koko scolded her. "You'll have to clean that up."

"It's not my fault," Tsune replied. "The water won't stay where I put it."

"What do you mean? You haven't put it anywhere yet."

"I put it in the bucket," Tsune said, pointing as if Oba Koko couldn't see.

"Well, never mind. We have someone to do that for you now. This is our new nephew. Show him where the well is. And where did Nui go? Is she hiding again? That's the laziest girl we've ever had here."

Seikei took the bucket from Tsune and poured the

rest of the water into a barrel standing in the corner. He didn't spill a drop. Hoping Oba Koko would notice, he turned around to meet only a resentful stare from Tsune. She thought he had done it to embarrass her.

"I need six more buckets of water," the cook said as Seikei started out the back door with Tsune. She led him into a courtyard that the teahouse shared with three other buildings—one next door and two that faced onto the street beyond. In the middle of the courtyard was a stone well, along with a few wooden sheds that looked as if they were used for storage.

As Seikei drew another bucket of water, Tsune said, "Don't work so fast. They'll just give you something else to do."

Seikei nodded. "Is there a lot of work to do?"

"Oh, everything. We're just like slaves, that's all. I had to come here because my mother died and my father couldn't afford to keep all of us. Since I was the oldest, I had to be sold."

"Sold? Really?"

"Well, they paid my father money and in return I'm supposed to work ten years. But Oba Koko says she adds on time for whatever I break or spoil or spill. She keeps a record, but I can't read it."

"How long have you been here?"

"Four years. Since I was nine. How come you're here? What happened to Kiru?"

"I was walking by when Oba Koko chased him out. I don't know why."

"She's always kicking him out. But then he begs to be let back, and she takes him. She doesn't like to have men or boys here—except the customers, of course. But sometimes she needs one. The customers can be difficult."

Seikei carried the bucket inside, careful not to spill the water. Tsune walked close behind him—too close. It seemed to Seikei as if she were trying to make him lose his balance.

But when he poured the water into the barrel, she only sighed, "I wish I knew how to do that." He realized she had been only trying to see how he carried the water.

"Don't get in nephew's way," the cook told her. "You can peel some onions."

Tsune groaned. Seikei thought he saw a tear fall from her eye before she'd even picked up an onion.

He went back outside. A flash of green silk caught his eye. Someone had ducked out of the way behind one of the small sheds in the courtyard.

Curious, he went around the opposite side and circled the shed. He saw another girl, squatting and peering toward the well.

He set the bucket down and she whirled around. She was a little younger than Tsune, but more importantly her face didn't seem to have so many complaints written on it. Seikei thought she was pretty.

"Oh! You frightened me!" she said. "I didn't know anyone was here."

He knew that wasn't true, since she had hidden from him. "I am the new nephew of Oba Koko," he said.

"Don't you have a real name?"

"Seikei."

She nodded. "I am Nui."

Now he understood why the girl was hiding. "Oba Koko was looking for you," he said.

She tossed her head and sniffed. "She only wants me to do some work."

Reminded of what *he* was supposed to be doing, Seikei went to the well and lowered the bucket. The girl followed, glancing around to see if anyone was watching.

"Aren't you *supposed* to be working?" Seikei asked her. "Oba Koko may throw you out if you don't."

"No, she won't," said Nui, sounding very sure of herself. "She paid my father a lot of money for me and she can't afford to lose it."

Seikei poured the water into the bucket he had carried. "I have to take this into the kitchen," he said. "But I'll be back for more."

She laughed. "Oh, you want me to wait for you?"

Stung, he shrugged and said, "If you wish."

"Promise to bring me a persimmon," she said, "and I will wait. The cook keeps them in a box near the door."

He didn't reply. He returned to the kitchen and poured the water, distracted by thoughts of Nui. Tsune was standing at a table, cutting onions and sniffing loudly, but Seikei barely noticed her. He had spotted the box of reddish-orange ripe persimmons.

The cook's back was turned and Tsune's eyes were full of tears. On the way out, Seikei's hand reached out as if it had a life of its own and plucked a persimmon from the box.

He stopped to rest in the corridor. His heart was pounding. He had never stolen anything before in his life. He didn't know what had made him do it.

Yes, he did, he admitted to himself. He wanted the girl to think he was brave enough to do it.

But what if someone caught him? He would surely be thrown out of the house, if not taken to the local magistrate. He would have disgraced himself.

Standing there, however, he remembered why the judge had wanted him to find work here. Seikei was to learn as much as he could about the murders of the geishas. Perhaps this girl, Nui, had more to tell him. Seikei should win her confidence. If the price of that was a persimmon, then it was justified.

In any case, no one seemed to have noticed that he

took it. He continued on to the courtyard. There he found the girl standing at the well staring down into it.

"I brought you the persimmon," said Seikei, holding it out to her.

She gave it only a brief glance. "Oh, I don't want it now," she said. "I just wanted to see if you would bring it."

Seikei's hand shook. He couldn't believe how foolish the girl had made him look. He put the persimmon in the sleeve of his jacket and pushed past her to lower the bucket again.

"Don't treat me so rudely," Nui said.

"Why not?"

"Or I'll tell Oba Koko that you're a thief."

Now he felt like flinging himself into the well.

"You asked me to bring it," he muttered helplessly.

"Why do you have your hair cut like a samurai?" she asked suddenly.

He resolved to keep silent. Let Nui try to provoke him further. That way, at least he might learn something.

"Oh," she said, when it became apparent he was not going to reply. "I think I can guess. In your heart, you probably wish to be a samurai."

Seikei pulled the rope of the bucket out of the well, hand over hand. He was surprised how easily Nui could read his thoughts. Perhaps she was the demon he was searching for.

"None of us can control our destiny," Nui said. She studied him further. "I do not think you are destined to become a samurai."

Seikei's face was hot with the effort it took him not to respond to the girl's taunts. He slipped his hand in the water and splashed a little on his cheeks.

"My destiny, though," she went on, "is to become a geisha. I'm sure of it. So is Oba Koko, which is why she won't ever dismiss me or sell me to another teahouse." She turned her back on Seikei and lowered the back of her kimono—just enough to show the base of her neck. "Look," she said. "Don't you think I am as beautiful as a geisha?"

That part of a woman's neck was regarded as the key to her beauty. Despite himself, Seikei looked. Nui's neck was as graceful as a swan's. He tried to force himself to look away, but couldn't.

She shrugged the garment into place again and turned to face him. Her brown eyes looked boldly into his. He felt she could make him steal an entire barrel of persimmons if she wished.

"After a geisha accepts me as her apprentice," she said, "I will make far more for Oba Koko than she could ever earn from this teahouse. But that isn't going to be enough for me. I want some daimyo—he must be very rich—to shower me with presents until I agree to give up being a geisha and marry him."

Just then, Oba Koko herself appeared at the doorway

at the back of the house. "Oh, there you are, Nui," she said. "I've been looking for you."

"I had to make sure this new nephew drew the water from the well properly," Nui replied. "I think he's very stupid, for he doesn't talk much."

"That's good because you talk *too* much," Oba Koko replied. "Now, both of you, come inside. The magistrate is here. He wants to question everyone in the house."

6

ANOTHER THIEF

*O*n the way back through the kitchen, Seikei let the persimmon slip from his sleeve into the box. He resolved not to let Nui tempt him into more trouble.

Oba Koko led the cook, Seikei, Nui, and Tsune into one of the tearooms. Judge Ooka and another man were seated in the place of honor in front of a scroll. The others all bowed and knelt on the floor.

"Are these all the members of the household?" the second man asked.

"There is only my aged mother, Lord," said Oba Koko. "But she is too frail to leave her room."

"What if there were a fire?" the man asked. "What would she do then?"

Oba Koko seemed surprised. "Why . . . we would carry her to safety," she said.

The man nodded. "You no doubt are all aware that I am Odozo, magistrate appointed by the shogun to extend his authority over the Yoshiwara district. Beside me is the shogun's official, Judge Ooka, who has informed me that a criminal of the most dangerous kind may be here in Yoshiwara."

Oba Koko gave a long cry of "ahhhhhh," which the cook and the two girls promptly imitated. Seikei realized he was supposed to show a similar sign of awe, so he did. Of course, he knew, no one was really surprised in the least.

"We have come to warn you to beware of any strange people in the district," Odozo went on. He gestured toward Oba Koko. "Can you account for all the people in your household?" he asked.

Nui glanced over her shoulder at Seikei, raising an eyebrow. Even now she was mocking him.

"I just hired this boy," said Oba Koko.

Judge Ooka broke in. "We will examine him carefully," he said. "In the meantime, I wish to caution all of you—do not accept any invitations to leave the teahouse with a stranger."

"Oh, no one would do that, Lord," said Oba Koko. "None of my nieces would do anything improper."

"They might not think the purpose of the invitation was improper," said the judge. "The danger would not be apparent until later."

"From now on," said Odozo, "every teahouse must keep a record of its customers and the geishas who invite customers here."

Oba Koko gave a low moan that sounded more sincere than her earlier cry of awe. And when the two girls tried to imitate it, she turned angrily and hushed them.

"Many customers do not wish their names to be known," Oba Koko pointed out. "They may even give false names."

"Even if the names are false, you will take them down," said Odozo. "I command it." He looked at Judge Ooka. Seikei thought he was silently asking if he should say anything else.

"The rest of you may go," said Judge Ooka. "But you shall remain," he said, pointing at Seikei.

Oba Koko looked unhappy. "He told me he was honest," she said. "I am not responsible for anything he's done."

The judge cut her off with a wave of his hand.

The sliding doors of the house did not offer much protection against being overheard. So after the others left, the judge motioned Seikei to move closer to himself and Odozo.

"I want you to remain here," the judge said in a low voice. "Stay alert for any signs of the criminal."

"Am I looking for a person who sets fires or one who kills geishas and teahouse girls?" Seikei asked.

"I believe that either one may lead to the other," said the judge.

Odozo interrupted. "We have no proof that anyone in Yoshiwara has been killed."

Judge Ooka nodded curtly. "When we find the killer, we will find the proof."

Odozo looked unhappy and turned his eyes toward Seikei. Seikei sensed that the local magistrate did not welcome the judge's assistance. Whatever they had discussed in private had not been pleasing to Odozo. "This boy does not look experienced," he said.

"He is observant," replied the judge. "And resourceful."

Seikei remembered what he had wanted to ask the judge. "If I see anything you should know," he asked, "how should I send a message?"

"You may report anything you see to Odozo," said the judge. "He can send a messenger to me."

Seikei looked at Odozo, who had pressed his lips tightly together, as if to keep himself from objecting.

"After your warning," Seikei told the judge, "the woman who owns the teahouse—Oba Koko—will be suspicious of me. She may even dismiss me. She seems to do that quite suddenly."

"I will tell her that we have examined and approved you," said the judge. "Odozo will recommend strongly that she keep you in the household for her protection."

Seikei smiled to himself when he thought of what the girl Nui would think if she heard that. But he added, "Oba Koko told me I should obey her in all things."

"Please her if you can," said the judge. "But remember what our purpose is. We must catch the person who is setting fires in Edo before any more of them occur."

Seikei wanted to ask what the connection was between the person who set the fires and the deaths of the three women in Yoshiwara. Aside from the kimono, there seemed no connection. But Seikei trusted that the judge must see the criminal's path more clearly than he did.

There were still more buckets of water to carry from the well to the kitchen, so Seikei went back to his duties. Nui had disappeared, but Tsune and the cook gave him odd looks as he brought the first bucket inside. Oba Koko entered the kitchen and followed him back to the courtyard.

"Stand right there a moment," she said.

Seikei stopped, wondering what she would say. Instead, she removed a folded paper cone from her kimono. Swiftly, she poured out a trail of salt onto the paving stones, making a circle around Seikei.

"Let's see you step over that," she said.

Seikei easily stepped out of the circle.

"Hm," Oba Koko said. "All right, but you still could be using some kind of magic."

"Oba Koko," Seikei said, "you pinched my nose, and now you tried the salt circle. You can't still think I'm a demon."

"Why not, I'd like to know?" she asked. "You think demons are always ugly looking?"

"Didn't Judge Ooka tell you he had examined me?"

"Pah," she said. "What does he know? I've heard about Judge Ooka. People say he can tell a guilty person just by smelling him. But I'll keep my eye on you, just the same. Anyone can be fooled, even that fat judge."

Seikei bit his tongue to keep from replying.

Oba Koko went on, "Don't think you're sleeping inside the house, no matter what the judge says. You'll be right in there, where Kiru and the other nephews have always stayed." She pointed to a small shed that had been added to the back of the house.

"But I can't protect you if I sleep there," he said.

"I'll sound an alarm if I need help," she replied. "Now hurry up with the water. I have to show you your duties before the evening guests arrive. And you'll need suitable clothes. All the employees wear matching kimonos or jackets."

When Seikei finished bringing the last bucket of water inside, the cook gave him a plate of rice and vegetables. Tsune, who had finished chopping onions and was now shelling walnuts, looked at him resentfully. Seikei felt awkward.

"Could Tsune have a bowl of rice too?" he asked the cook.

"She'll get something when she's finished her work,"

the cook replied. "If you feed the horse before you harness it, it won't plow the furrow."

Seikei remembered his father the merchant saying something like that.

"Besides," added the cook, "you won't have time to eat again until the guests leave. And we have to keep you strong so you can protect us." She laughed at the thought, and his face reddened.

The food was good, Seikei found. As he ate, he looked up for a moment and found Tsune's eyes on him. She smiled and nodded, and he realized she was grateful that he had asked the cook to give her a bowl.

When he finished his meal, Oba Koko showed him the rest of the teahouse. There were three large party rooms for as many as twelve people, and smaller rooms where geishas might meet a few favorite customers.

"The most important geisha we will have tonight is Umae," said Oba Koko. "But you should only go in her room if she calls you. Nui and Tsune will bring anything necessary from the kitchen."

"Then what will I be needed for?"

"What I told you before. Be ready to throw someone out if they become too rowdy."

Seikei nodded, hoping that wouldn't happen often.

Oba Koko saw his doubts. "It's not up to you to decide," she added. "One of the geishas will signal you if she wants help. Mostly the guests become so drunk that they need help going to the privy or getting out the front door. Call a *kago* to take them back to the ferry to Edo. The night air will revive them, but if not, they are someone else's worry."

"They need help going to the privy?" Seikei asked. He didn't like the sound of that.

"Yes. It's outside next to the hut where you sleep. Make sure they don't fall in. There is always a terrible fuss from the authorities when that happens."

Oba Koko waved her hand. "I must prepare," she said. "Change out of your clothes. You'll find a suitable outfit in the shed where you sleep."

Seikei went there, to find that the shed was dark. The only light came from a missing slat covered with rice paper. A rolled-up *tatami* sleeping mat rested against one wall. Inside a plain wooden chest, he found two sets of plum-colored pantaloons and jackets, decorated only with strips of white linen. They hadn't been folded carefully, and as Seikei examined them, he found that they needed washing as well.

No one seemed to have anything else for him to do just now. So he went outside and drew a bucket of water from the well. The cook let him have some orange peels that he added to the water. Using a scrub brush, he washed one of the outfits. Wringing out the two pieces of clothing, he hung them to dry on a pole.

He went back inside the shed, leaving the door open to air it out. His duties at the teahouse seemed ideal for what the judge wanted him to do. If all went well, he could sit quietly and observe the guests. If only he were as shrewd as Judge Ooka, he could pick out the criminal.

The judge had once told Seikei that a criminal was someone who was like a pine tree that had grown up twisted and misshapen by the wind. "Most people wish to live in harmony with others," the judge often said. "They know that is the best way to have order and peace. But the criminal violates that harmony for some reason. It may seem like a good reason—to him. If you find that reason, you find the criminal."

What reason could there be for killing geishas? Geishas were, after all, only entertainers. They learned to please and amuse their customers. A geisha who caused someone to want to kill her would be noticed. She certainly would not find work in Yoshiwara.

And the connection between the geishas and the fires? That was even more puzzling. Whoever set a fire deliberately must be a very evil person indeed. Many people might die, and surely many others would lose their homes and shops. People in Edo still spoke fearfully of the Great Furisode Fire. It had swept through Edo many years ago, in the time of Emperor Gosai. Over one hundred thousand people had died, many of them trampled to death as people tried to save themselves by running to the rivers and moats.

Suddenly Seikei realized that the light in the hut had faded. The sun had set, and he was sitting in darkness. It was time for him to get dressed for his evening's duties. He got up and went outside, where there was enough twilight to let him see clearly—clearly enough to see that the jacket and pantaloons he had hung up to dry were now gone. He could hardly believe it. He looked around to see if they might have blown off the pole.

Then he became angry. Only one person would have been mean enough to steal his clothes. He stormed into the teahouse to find her.

7

A STRANGE ENCOUNTER

*W*here is Nui?" Seikei asked the cook.

She looked at him strangely. "Why?" she asked.

He hesitated. He didn't want to announce the fact that his clothes had been stolen. That would only cause more amusement about the boy who was supposed to "protect" them.

He turned his anger on himself: It was clearly his own carelessness that had allowed Nui to steal his clothes. He had been taken in by her beauty, failing to see what her true character was. From now on he would be more vigilant.

"Did she come through the kitchen recently?" he asked.

"No," the cook replied. "She is upstairs with Tsune. They are dressing. It is about time you did too."

Since Oba Koko had forbidden Seikei to go upstairs, there was nothing he could do. He went back to the shed. The only other garments that would fit him were wrinkled and stained. He had no time to wash and dry them, but he wiped some of the spots away with a damp cloth.

Seikei changed into the teahouse outfit quickly. Then he folded his own clothes and put them inside the rolled-up tatami mat as a hiding place. Of course, while he was gone, anyone might search the shed and easily find them. But it was the best he could do.

When he returned to the kitchen, the cook looked him over critically. "I thought you were going to wash those clothes," she said.

He mumbled an excuse. "The other outfit is still wet."

"You should have wrung it out thoroughly," the cook said. "You look even worse than Kiru did. I wouldn't have thought that possible."

He bowed his head in embarrassment. "I will do better tomorrow," he said.

"Well, stay in a dark corner so no one sees you. The geishas don't like it if the teahouse doesn't appear high class."

"Can I do anything to help now?"

"Take that pole and light the lanterns on the front porch."

Seikei picked up a long wooden pole that had a candle tied to one end. He lit it at the stove and then went through the house. Along the roof of the front porch hung colored paper lanterns. Seikei carefully lit the candles inside each one, and as he did, their red, blue, and green shades burst into bloom like flowers in the night.

All up and down the street, other lanterns were being lit. Their brilliant colors made the street seem as if a merry festival were about to begin. The pine resin of the candles gave off a sweet scent. Servants hurried along, carrying jugs of *sake,* trays of candies, and bags of fruit for the evening's parties.

A kago came down the street, carried by two burly men. It reminded Seikei of the passenger-box he used to ride in when he was the son of a merchant. This one was grander than that, however. It was decorated with yellow watered silk and small pieces of stone or shell that reflected the colored lanterns.

To his surprise, the kago-bearers set it down in front of the teahouse. A door slid aside and the most beautiful woman Seikei had ever seen got out.

She was, of course, a geisha. Her face was covered with white makeup that emphasized her bright red lips, the large eyes outlined in black, and the delicate eyebrows that had been drawn high on her forehead. A thick black wig covered her head, with several *kanzashi* sticking out of it. These were exquisitely decorated hairpins made of ivory, silver, and rare, beautiful kinds of wood.

The kago was close to the front steps of the teahouse. The geisha made three tiny steps forward. Then she gathered up the bottom of the kimono so she could lift her foot onto the step. The cloth was heavy, Seikei could see, because it was thick brocade embroidered with a multitude of flowers.

Suddenly the door to the teahouse opened and Oba Koko rushed out. "*Irasshaimase!* Welcome!" she cried. "Our house is honored by your presence, Umae." Oba Koko bowed low and offered a hand for the geisha to take if she needed help coming up the steps.

Umae ignored the offered hand. It seemed to Seikei that the geisha didn't wish Oba Koko to disturb the graceful way she was ascending the steps.

Then Oba Koko noticed Seikei. "Aiiii!" she called. "Out of the way, stupid boy. Run and tell Nui that Umae has arrived."

Seikei had not been blocking Umae's path at all. But he did as he was told.

Umae was perhaps the most famous geisha in Edo. No one knew how old she really was, for her makeup was so skillfully applied that she could be any age. She was even more renowned for her talents at entertaining. Seikei hoped he would be able to observe her performance that night.

Inside, he nearly collided with Nui, who was just coming down the stairs. She too had dressed in a plum-colored kimono bearing the crest of the teahouse. But her outfit was as splendid and fresh as his was shabby, and she wore a contrasting white obi that made her seem even more beautiful. The sight of her nearly made Seikei forget that she had taken his freshly washed clothes.

It was impossible to bring that up now. "Umae has arrived," he told her.

Nui's eyes sparkled with joy. "Stay out of the way, if you can," she ordered him brusquely. "I want Umae to think favorably of the teahouse."

Seikei choked back a retort. He wanted to say he would look much better if someone had not stolen his clothing. Instead, he strode angrily toward the back of the house, where he failed to notice the kitchen door slide open. As Tsune emerged with a tray of sweets, he bumped into her. The tray nearly fell, but she managed to catch it.

"Watch out!" she said.

He apologized, and she told him, "That's all right. Everyone is on edge because Umae is coming."

"She is already here," Seikei said. "Both Oba Koko and Nui acted as if I were a frog at a tea party."

"They want to make a good impression because Nui hopes to become Umae's younger sister."

Seikei was puzzled. "You mean be adopted by her?"

"No. To become a younger sister means Nui would become Umae's apprentice. The only way to become a geisha is for one to take you as a younger sister. Because Umae is so highly respected, Nui would become famous—and, of course, Oba Koko would get part of her earnings."

"I see," said Seikei.

"Can I tell you a secret?" asked Tsune.

"Of course." Perhaps this would be important information, the kind the judge wanted Seikei to discover.

"I have a dream of my own."

Seikei blinked. "You do?" he said. "You want to be a geisha too?" Seikei didn't say so, but he couldn't imagine that ever happening.

"No," Tsune said, putting her hand over her mouth to hide a smile. "Geishas have to please men. That's all they do. Even when they're not *with* men, they're making themselves more beautiful or improving their skills at singing and dancing. I wouldn't want to do that."

"Still . . . ," Seikei began, thinking of what Nui had said earlier, ". . . they make a lot of money."

"You talk like a merchant," Tsune said.

Seikei's face grew hot, for that stung him more than Tsune realized.

"No," she continued, "*my* dream is to own a teahouse like this one. Perhaps this very one," she said, looking around. "Oba Koko will not live forever."

Seikei was surprised. "Well," he pointed out, "you'd still have to please men."

"No one is completely free," admitted Tsune, "but beauty fades. Someday even Umae will have to retire. And even with all the money she earns now, I think she will be lonely then. Oba Koko, on the other hand, can hire new geishas anytime. She takes care of her elderly mother—and she has plenty of people to boss around. Who wouldn't envy her?"

Seikei shook his head. He reflected that Tsune was wiser than she appeared.

Before long, guests started to arrive. Umae had sent out messages that she had chosen the Teahouse of the Falling Cherry Blossoms as her new place to entertain. Her special customers followed.

Seikei finally found a place where he could observe the guests without being in the way. There was a small room off the main hall that was used by geishas who wanted to adjust their makeup or clothing. Leaving the door open a crack, Seikei could see Oba Koko welcoming guests.

The first to arrive had rented a large straw hat at the shops by the ferry. When he removed it, Seikei saw why he had wished to conceal his identity. It was Genda, one of the officials at the shogun's court. Seikei had seen him a few times at the judge's Edo residence. Genda was one of the *ometsuke,* whose task it was to spy on other officials to discover wrongdoing.

Making a trip to the teahouses at Yoshiwara was not a violation of the law. But it was well known that the shogun frowned on the practice. He feared that those who did it could become so involved in the pursuit of pleasure that they would neglect their duties.

Yet here was Genda. Well, thought Seikei, that would

be interesting to the judge. Because Genda was envious. He wanted the respect that people felt for the judge. As a result, he was always in search of some fault or mistake of the judge's that Genda could report to the shogun. The judge was not bothered. "It is Genda's job to do this," he told Seikei. "And like everyone else, I should not be exempt from criticism or suspicion."

But Seikei knew that Bunzo and the judge's other samurai retainers detested Genda. They would be grateful if Seikei could find some misconduct on his part. Attending a teahouse was not exactly misconduct, but it was certainly unworthy of an official who wanted to please the shogun.

Not long afterward, another guest arrived. He wore no disguise. With his hair tied in a topknot, he was clearly a samurai, even though he'd been obliged to leave his swords at the gatehouse. Seikei overheard Oba Koko call him Jugoro. He was young, handsome, and looked the way Seikei imagined a heroic samurai must.

After Oba Koko escorted Jugoro to the room where Umae was, she returned to the main hallway. Seikei was startled when she suddenly slid open the door to his hiding place. "What are you doing there, lazy nephew?" she asked angrily. She did not raise her voice, however, and Seikei realized she would not make a fuss that might disturb the guests.

"You told me to stay out of the way, Auntie," said Seikei. "I wanted to be ready in case I could be useful."

"Eh, you have a clever tongue," she said. "But as it happens I do have something for you to do." She handed him a note. "I am afraid we will have too many guests for Umae to entertain by herself. Take this to the next street west, third house from the far end on the right side. Give it to the girl who answers the door, but tell her I want Maiko to see it at once. Do you understand?"

"Yes," said Seikei.

"Come back right away and don't dawdle," she told him.

Outside, the street was crowded now. Partygoers, some of them in groups, strolled up and down, laughing and discussing which teahouse would have the best entertainment. Some geishas walked along too, taking small delicate steps in their geta.

It wasn't difficult for Seikei to find his way to the place Oba Koko had described. There were only five streets in Yoshiwara. The house where he was supposed to go was not a business. He supposed it was one of the places where the geishas lived when they were not working. He had heard that some spent their whole lives in Yoshiwara, never going to other parts of Edo. At the door a girl took the note and told him she would give it to Maiko.

On the way back, Seikei looked behind him a few times to see if anyone was following. When Seikei had helped the judge solve the mystery of a stolen jewel, the judge had sent Bunzo in disguise to follow him. Seikei thought it likely that Bunzo was nearby now, but he couldn't pick him out of the crowd.

Unfortunately, not watching where he was going, Seikei bumped into someone. The other person pushed him out of the way with an angry grunt. Seikei began to apologize to the man, whose tied-topknot hairstyle, jacket, and trousers marked him as a samurai. However, he had allowed his beard and mustache to grow, something unusual for a samurai. Though the man was slightly built, only a little heavier than Seikei, his eyes looked fierce. Seikei was glad that all visitors to Yoshiwara had to surrender their swords.

Before Seikei could get away, the man caught him by the arm. "That jacket you wear," he said. "Where did you get it?"

Seikei looked down. He had almost forgotten about his new clothing. "Why . . . from my auntie at the tea-house," he said.

"The Teahouse of the Falling Cherry Blossoms?"

"Yes. How did you know?"

"I recognize the pattern. No matter. Is it true that Umae has chosen it as her new teahouse for entertaining guests?"

"Yes," Seikei said. "It is a great honor for us."

The man smiled, but his eyes continued to drill into Seikei as if searching for something. "Perhaps I will see you there later," he said.

With that, he released Seikei's arm and went off in the other direction.

Seikei returned to the teahouse, wondering about the strange encounter. Perhaps he should not have answered the samurai's question. But why not? Oba Koko would be glad if Seikei had attracted another customer. There must be many men who followed Umae from one teahouse to another. Genda and Jugoro certainly had.

But the memory of the bearded samurai made Seikei uneasy. There was something about the way his eyes looked that seemed . . . Seikei could not name it, but he had no wish to look into them again soon.

8

THE KIMONO RETURNS

By the Hour of the Pig, when one day changed to another, the teahouse was filled with people. Oba Koko's message, which Seikei had delivered, had brought two other geishas, Maiko and Odori. Oba Koko needed them to handle the overflow of customers who had arrived as the news spread that Umae was entertaining here. All three rooms in the teahouse were open.

Seikei was busy now. He had to help Tsune bring trays of food and jugs of sake from the kitchen. From time to time, Oba Koko summoned him to guide customers to the rooms where Maiko and Odori were entertaining. This was difficult, for most of those who came through the front door wanted to see Umae. Seikei had to promise that they could, just as soon as there was space in her room.

Whenever he had the chance, he stopped to watch the geishas. Though Maiko and Odori were not so beautiful as Umae, he enjoyed their performances. Maiko strummed her three-stringed *samisen* and sang songs that took the listeners into times long past. She sang of tragic lovers and the deeds of brave but doomed heroes. Seikei noticed that the customers in Maiko's room drank more sake than those in the other rooms.

Odori, on the other hand, was fun loving and jolly. She told jokes that got the customers into a good mood. Then she organized games in which the loser had to pay a penalty. Not money—that would be vulgar and remind the customers of the real world beyond the floating world of Yoshiwara. Odori made the losers do something comical, like imitate frogs or tilt a cup of sake from their noses to their mouths.

Seikei was amazed at the way everyone took their penalties with good humor. Proud samurai and powerful daimyos were happily leaping over each others' backs, crouching on the floor trying to croak like frogs, or laughing at their own clumsiness as cups of sake spilled over their faces.

In Umae's room, things were quieter. She had selected most of the guests herself. Besides the samurai Jugoro and Genda the ometsuke, there were several elderly daimyos who had apparently known Umae for years. Two or three others—wealthy merchants who had slipped Oba Koko "thank-money" for the privilege—had been allowed to sit at the far end of the room.

Umae had developed all the skills a geisha should

have. She had a lovely singing voice, accompanying herself on the samisen. If she wished, she could tell stories that made the listeners weep one moment or burst into laughter the next. Her beauty and grace were such that men enjoyed merely watching her pour tea or offer a plate of sweets.

Seikei had little chance to observe her. For most of the night he had been kept busy carrying tea trays and barrels of sake, cleaning spills from the floor, and— once—helping to revive a customer who had fallen into a deep sleep.

Then Oba Koko summoned him to help one of the elderly daimyos from Umae's room to the privy in the rear courtyard. The old man was standing in the corridor outside Umae's room, leaning unsteadily against the wall. Seikei realized that was the only thing keeping him upright. A couple of laughing young samurai brushed past the old man on their way toward the front door, and Seikei had to catch him before he toppled.

Surprisingly, the daimyo wasn't very heavy. He felt like a bundle of dry sticks. He was able to walk, however. And as Seikei half led, half carried him down the hallway, the man hummed some high-pitched tune to himself. Whoever the demon was, Seikei was pretty sure this was not the man the judge wanted him to find.

The air in the courtyard felt cool and fresh after the crowded teahouse. It even revived the daimyo a little. He was able to stumble into the privy by himself. Seikei was thankful. As he waited, he could hear laughter and music from all the windows of the teahouses along the alley. Even though a demon was at large, the residents of Yoshiwara kept up the cheerful spirit of the floating world. For that was why customers came here—to forget trouble, not to encounter it.

The daimyo emerged, tying the obi of his kimono closed. He took Seikei's arm, for it was dark out here and the stones underfoot made walking hazardous. Seikei felt him pat his shoulder. "Youth," said the daimyo. "So blind, so blind."

Seikei thought this was something of an unkind comment, since he was leading the daimyo, not the other way around.

"You know Umae?" asked the man. "Have you fallen in love with her?"

"No," Seikei replied, trying to be polite. "This is the first time I have seen her."

"Ah, beware then, beware," said the daimyo. "She is alluring . . . but if you let her steal your heart, you are lost."

"I won't do that," Seikei said.

The daimyo continued, as if he hadn't heard. "A geisha like her . . . she demands presents, you know. I have known men who lost their heads trying to please a geisha."

Little danger of that, thought Seikei. I have nothing to give. Then he remembered what had happened that afternoon. When he stole a persimmon just because Nui had asked him to. Was that the kind of power geishas had over men?

They entered the house and made their way down the corridor. "Yes," the daimyo said, talking more to himself than to Seikei. "Beauty can hide a cruel heart. Men have lost fortunes . . . and even their honor . . . and still they persist."

It was awkward for Seikei to release the daimyo outside the room where Umae was. Instead, he helped him through the doorway and back to the place he had apparently occupied earlier.

Seikei slipped into the shadows near the back wall and sat down. He was curious, and if no one noticed, he wanted to feel the allure of Umae. She was seated at the head of the table, of course. A scroll on the wall behind her displayed a poem by the famous samurai poet Basho and a painting of fallen cherry blossoms.

Seikei knew well the meaning of the cherry blossoms. In the spring they bloom in great abundance on the trees. But their time is short. Soon a wind or sudden storm inevitably comes and takes them away, scattering their loveliness upon the ground.

In the same way, life itself lasts for but a moment in eternity. Men and women in their turn bloom, display their beauty, and then fall. Is life beautiful? Or sad? The cherry blossom reminds us that it is both.

Somehow, Umae's beauty seemed to defy the inevitable. Everyone knew that she was older than most other geishas. Yet her loveliness seemed untouched by time. Seikei couldn't have guessed her age. As she chatted with the men at the table, she looked still young and fresh. The gesture of putting her hand over her mouth as she laughed made her seem as innocent as a girl.

Seikei tore his eyes away to look at the others in the room. Nui sat off to Umae's side, watching her as closely as a cat. Seikei saw that Nui moved her hands in unison with Umae's, trying to duplicate her delicacy.

But no one else noticed. Sitting at the table on either side of Umae were Jugoro, the samurai, and Ometsuke Genda. They were clearly rivals for her attention. Jugoro was pouring sake into Umae's cup while Genda playfully pretended to be hiding something in his sleeve. He kept peering inside it and then pulling his arm away when Umae tried to see what he was concealing.

Quietly, the door slid open and another man stepped inside. Seikei recognized him at once as the bearded samurai he'd met in the street earlier. No one paid him any attention until Umae looked up.

She seemed a little annoyed. "Have you come to join our party?" she said lightly.

The bearded samurai didn't reply. He sat down next to one of the old daimyos at the end of the table and gestured to Nui that he wanted sake.

"I think this stranger is quite rude," said the samurai Jugoro. "He does not even give his name."

Genda glared at the bearded man. "Send him away, Umae," he urged. As a tayu, Umae did have the right to refuse a customer. Seikei wondered what the bearded samurai's reaction would be if she did.

Before she could respond, however, the stranger said, "I merely brought a gift for the geisha who calls herself Umae."

Umae turned to Nui and said, "Pour him sake. Why are you hesitating?"

Embarrassed, Nui rushed to do as she was told. The bearded samurai raised the cup, said, *"Kampai!"* and tossed down the sake.

Umae sipped a little from her own cup. "Do I know you?" she asked.

"We have never met before," he replied. "But your reputation carries far."

She smiled politely.

"Of course, I do not know if you really are Umae," the man said.

Jugoro and Genda laughed loudly and the old daimyos joined in. "Everyone knows she's Umae," said Jugoro, "but we don't have *your* name yet."

"I have heard," said the man, "that in the floating world one can become whoever one chooses to be."

"Well, that's if you want to playact," said Genda. "You can dress up and find geishas who will pretend with you. Kabuki actors often come here too. But at least they have names."

"You can call me Fukushu," the man said.

There was an uneasy silence in the room for a moment. Fukushu meant *revenge.*

"I don't like that name," Umae said in a girlish voice. "It's unpleasant. It doesn't belong in Yoshiwara."

"Tell him to leave," growled Genda again. He waved his hand at the stranger, as if trying to brush him out of the room. "He's spoiling our fun." Suddenly Genda spotted Seikei seated by the wall. "You!" he said, pointing. "Don't you work for the teahouse? Show this man where the street is."

Seikei tensed. The bearded samurai wasn't a very large man, but he looked wiry. Unlike most of the others in the room, he didn't seem to have been drinking all evening. If he didn't want to leave, Seikei would have a hard time forcing him to.

However, the bearded samurai spoke in a mild tone. "I have not yet given Umae her present."

"Oh yes," said Jugoro mockingly, "let's see what kind of gift the noble Fukushu has brought."

"I will need your help," said the bearded samurai, nodding at Seikei.

As Seikei stood, the room resounded with laughter. The guests made humorous suggestions as to what the gift could be:

"Must be something heavy!"

"Maybe an anchor for a boat?"

"No, he looks more like a monk than a sailor . . . so it's probably a statue of the Buddha."

"Could be a horse! Do you count riding among your talents, Umae?"

The bearded samurai ignored the jeers. He beckoned for Seikei to follow him. They went to the front hallway. There, resting under the household shrine, was a beautifully wrapped box. A blue silk cord secured the wrapping of fine rice paper with a hand-painted design of a forest scene. It was one of those wrapped presents that look so beautiful, one doesn't want to open it.

"It's not so large," Seikei pointed out. It was in fact no bigger than a couple of tatami mats rolled together.

"You can easily carry it by yourself," the bearded samurai agreed. "Present it to the geisha Umae with my regards. Tell her I hope to see her again."

With that, he went out into the night. Seikei's impulse was to follow him. But what for? He had done nothing wrong, and there was no way Seikei could keep up with him without being seen.

Anyway, Seikei was curious to learn what was inside the package. As he picked it up, he realized that it was lighter than he expected. The box was made of cardboard and whatever was inside fitted snugly enough not to rattle.

He brought it back to Umae's room and set it on the

floor next to her. "Where's the generous gift giver?" asked Jugoro.

"He left," explained Seikei. Turning to Umae, he added, "He told me to present this to you with his regards. Also, to tell you he hopes to see you again."

"Can't show his face after Umae sees the gift, eh?" said Genda with a snort. "That tells you what it must be like."

Umae took her time opening it. She exclaimed over the beauty and taste of the wrapping. The recipient of a gift always did this to be polite, it was true. But since the giver wasn't even there, Seikei thought her sentiments must be genuine.

At last, she pulled one end of the silken cord. Its elaborate knot fell apart and the paper fell away. The box itself was a plain white color. Umae moved it onto her lap and lifted the lid.

As she stared at the contents, she gave a little cry. Those around the room could see the box held something made of silk. Umae put her hands on it, as if to make sure it was real. She clutched the folds of cloth for a moment, and then pushed the box away, as if it contained something foul.

What lay inside was a beautiful silk kimono. It was the color of maple leaves in autumn. Embroidered on it in gold were cranes in flight, as if going south for the winter. Seikei recognized it at once, for he had already heard it described twice before.

9

BAD LUCK

*U*mae was so upset that she announced she was going home. Everyone wanted to know why the present had disturbed her. Genda angrily turned to Seikei.

"What happened to that samurai?" Genda demanded.

"He left," Seikei explained. Genda stared at Seikei for a second, and Seikei had the feeling the ometsuke recognized him. Genda thrust him aside and rushed out of the room, evidently intending to go after the man who called himself "Revenge."

Now Jugoro began to question Seikei. "Why is Umae upset?" he asked. "What was in that box?"

"Only a kimono," Seikei said. He decided it was better to say nothing about where he had heard of it before. The others began to plead with Umae to stay, but of course the party had been spoiled by now.

Just then Genda reappeared, a little out of breath. "He's gone," said Genda. "There is no sign of him." He turned to Seikei. "Do you know that man's real name?"

Genda seemed suspicious when Seikei replied honestly that he didn't know. "Then why did he give the present to you?" Genda asked.

"Only because he wanted to leave before it was opened, I suppose."

Oba Koko rushed into the room. "What's the matter?" she cried. "Umae has sent for her kago-bearers. Has someone offended her?" Spying Seikei, she said, "You were supposed to expel anyone who became unruly."

Seikei started to explain, but Nui interrupted. "He brought Umae a present that upset her," she announced.

"Where's my broomstick?" shouted Oba Koko. "Get out, stupid boy, before I—"

"Stop it!" Everyone turned. Umae stood in the doorway. It was she who had spoken. "It was not his fault. I apologize for ending the party so soon. Please . . ." She bowed to Jugoro and the other guests. "Come back soon when I am feeling more like myself. I do not want to laugh anymore tonight."

She looked at Seikei. "Take the present and burn it. It holds a bad memory for me, and I do not wish to see it again."

Seikei nodded, hurrying to close the lid of the box. Before he did so, he saw Oba Koko's sharp eyes flicker over the kimono.

Tsune came to announce that the kago had arrived, and Umae left, followed by Jugoro. Oba Koko turned to the old daimyos and said, "Come to one of the other rooms where Maiko and Odori are. For the rest of the evening, food and drinks are free."

Nui raised her eyebrows, for such generosity was unusual. As soon as Oba Koko escorted the guests into the corridor, Seikei angrily confronted Nui. "You knew I had nothing to do with that gift," he said. "Why did you accuse me?"

She sniffed. "How do I know you had nothing to do with it? We don't know anything about you. You frightened Umae, that's all I know. If I am going to be her little sister, I must make sure she enjoys coming to this teahouse."

Seikei spread his hands. "I only brought her a present that the samurai told me to deliver. How was I supposed to know it would upset her?"

Nui gave him an angry look. "I don't believe you. You must have known that samurai." She stamped her foot. "Either that or you are very stupid." With that, she swept out of the room.

Seikei picked up the box with the kimono. The judge would want to see this, he thought. It showed that the bearded samurai must have known the teahouse girl who drowned—perhaps he was even the one who killed her. Seikei shivered as he thought of the man's penetrating gaze. Another thought ran through his mind then: The bearded samurai might indeed be a demon in disguise.

Seikei took the box to the kitchen, thinking he would conceal it in the little hut in the courtyard. If anyone asked, he could say he burned it in the kitchen fireplace. Before he could get outside, however, Oba Koko caught up with him.

"Aii! Let's not be too hasty," she said. "That kimono . . . it looks valuable." She took the box from him and opened it. Lifting the kimono out, she held it up, letting it open to its full length. "Look how beautiful!" she said. "Truly something only a tayu would wear. It would be a shame to destroy it. Umae might change her mind later and ask for it back."

"But what if she . . . saw it later and learned I didn't burn it?" Seikei protested.

Oba Koko waved a hand as if brushing away a gnat. "These geishas . . . I know them better than you do. They never know what they really want." She folded the kimono neatly and replaced it in the box. "I'll just put this in a safe place," she said. She winked at him. "Trust me. She'll never know."

Seikei made some feeble noises of protest, but realized that even if he won the argument, he would have to burn the kimono as Oba Koko watched.

Word of Umae's departure had spread to the other parties in the teahouse. As Oba Koko and Seikei stepped back into the corridor, they saw most of the guests leaving. Oba Koko rushed to try to persuade them to stay.

Tsune came up to Seikei and asked, "Is it true that you brought an evil charm from the demon to Umae?"

"It wasn't anything like that!" protested Seikei.

"The guests don't want to stay in a house where the demon has been," Tsune pointed out.

It was true. Once a few of them started to leave, the rest followed. There was nobody left but a merchant in Maiko's room who had had too much to drink and had fallen asleep.

To make matters worse, the two geishas were afraid to go home by themselves. They could not afford a private kago, like Umae's.

"If the demon has returned to Yoshiwara," said Maiko, "it isn't safe for us to be outside this late."

Odori nodded. There was no playful smile on her face now.

Oba Koko pointed to Seikei. "You caused this. You can accompany Maiko and Odori home."

The two young geishas looked dismayed. "But he is the one who—" Odori began.

"He is not a demon," Oba Koko said. Without warning she reached out and pinched Seikei's nose again.

He let out a cry of pain. It hurt worse than the first time.

She ignored him. "You see? That proves he is not a demon."

"But he brought the charm."

"It was only a kimono," said Oba Koko. She opened

the box to show them. "It was all an unfortunate mis-understanding. Umae will return tomorrow night, and I expect to see you here too."

The two geishas looked doubtful, but Oba Koko urged them out the door. "You have nothing to worry about," she said. "This nephew of mine is very trust-worthy."

She leaned closed to Seikei and whispered in a voice no one else could hear. "If you let anything happen to them, you better go ask the demon for help . . . be-cause you'll have more to fear from me than from him."

Seikei believed her.

Outside, the streets were much quieter and darker than they had been earlier. In a few teahouses, parties were still going on. But many had closed their doors and extinguished the lanterns that hung outside.

Two samurai, singing arm in arm, swayed past them headed for the ferryboat back to Edo. They greeted the geishas too loudly, paying no attention to Seikei.

Odori and Maiko held hands as they walked, staying as far away from Seikei as possible. Little good that would do them, he thought, if he *had* been the demon.

They jumped when they heard a thumping noise coming from the far end of the street. All three of them froze for a second until they realized it was the sound of a horse's hooves. Its straw horseshoes pounding on the packed earth of the street sounded louder at night. As the horse drew nearer, they saw that the rider was one of the magistrate's patrol, a *doshin*. He gave them barely a glance as he passed by. If he were looking for wrongdoers, two young geishas and a teahouse servant were not likely suspects.

When the doshin had passed, Maiko asked Odori, "Are you going back there tomorrow night?"

"I don't think it's a good idea," came the reply. "Have you noticed?"

"Yes. It's clear that working with Umae brings bad luck."

The brief conversation made Seikei curious. He waited for them to say more, but they didn't.

"Why do you say that?" he asked finally.

They looked at him and drew another step farther away.

"I meant nothing by it," said Maiko. Her face froze into a mask.

He wanted to tell them that he was helping Judge Ooka investigate—that they should tell him whatever they knew. But that was impossible to say, and why would they believe him anyway?

"I apologize for my rudeness," he said. "But I have only just started to work at the teahouse. I had no other way to earn money. But if it is dangerous to work there, I must leave."

"It's not the teahouse," Odori said. She was the nicer of the two. "It's Umae."

"What's wrong with her? She was kind to me."

"Bad luck follows her," replied Odori.

"And death," Maiko said through clenched teeth.

The word hung in the air as they turned into the street where the geishas lived. It was even darker here, and now the women walked closer to Seikei.

"Umae used to work with two other tayu," said Odori. "Their names were Kimi and Satsu. Every tea-house wanted them to host parties there, because wealthy and powerful customers would follow wherever they went. And the gifts the three of them received! A fine kimono, you know, can cost more than an ordinary merchant makes in a year. So those who came to their parties had to be very wealthy."

"But so much success made others jealous," said Maiko darkly.

"That's what people say," admitted Odori. "Even though I was happy for them. Whenever one geisha prospers, so does Yoshiwara. But according to what I've heard, someone cast a spell—"

"—Or paid to have one cast," put in Maiko.

"—and a demon came here."

Silence fell again. Seikei jumped when something ran out from under a building and scurried across the street. It was only a rat, but he picked up a stone and threw it to conceal his fear.

"Did you ever see the demon?" he asked.

"Oh no," said Odori. "I wouldn't be here now if I had. I would have run away and become a Buddhist nun."

"So how do you know?"

"First," she began, "Kimi died. They found her in bed. Everyone said she'd been poisoned, because her tongue was swollen."

"People thought perhaps she ate some *fugu* that hadn't been properly cleaned," Maiko added. Fugu was a fish that was a great delicacy. However, its liver had to be carefully removed, for it was poisonous. "But Kimi had a delicate stomach and was always very careful about what she ate," she continued. "And no one else who had eaten with her the night before became ill."

"Then Satsu decided to go into Edo to visit her mother," Odori went on. "And she was killed in a fire."

"A fire?" Seikei couldn't help exclaiming.

"Yes. There have been several fires in Edo lately. Terrible . . . I hope we never have one here."

"But you think the demon caused the fire?" asked Seikei. "Just to kill Satsu?"

"Many people escaped the fire," Odori pointed out, "but Satsu did not. People here understood what that meant."

"Finally there was the teahouse servant," said Maiko.

"Bad luck," added Odori, shaking her head. "After the deaths of Kimi and Satsu, Umae had to find a new teahouse and she chose that one. The girl was nice to her, and see what happened. She wanted to become Umae's younger sister, I suppose. They are all like that."

Seikei thought of Nui.

"So the demon threw her in the river," Maiko said. "Well, Oba Koko may be foolish enough to allow Umae into her teahouse, but after tonight . . . I would not want to take the chance."

"Why wouldn't the demon kill Umae," asked Seikei, "if it's she that he's after?"

"She may have some magic of her own. You don't stay looking as young as she does without some tricks up your sleeve."

"But it doesn't protect those around her," said Maiko.

Odori nodded. "And so, if you please," she told Seikei, "give our best regards to Oba Koko, but tell her we cannot return tomorrow."

They had arrived at the house where the two geishas lived. They bowed politely and Seikei returned the gesture. "Be careful of yourself," Odori warned. "There is no reason why the demon would not kill you too. Even if you were his messenger, you have seen him, and that could be dangerous."

After Seikei left them, he wished she hadn't said that. All the shadows along the street now seemed to conceal lurking figures. A pair of candles burning low looked like fiery eyes watching him. When the moon went behind a cloud, he wished he had someplace to hide too.

Even a loud burst of laughter that broke the silence sounded like the cry of a demon, though it was only a guest who had stayed too late at a party. Seikei knew that some teahouses remained open till dawn, when the very last revelers would make their way across the bridge that linked the floating world to their ordinary lives.

As Seikei entered the main street again, he saw three samurai stumbling along, laughing and holding each other up. They stopped in front of a teahouse and shouted, but no one opened the door to greet them. Probably they had been asked to leave another one where they had worn out their welcome.

He hurried past them, although their presence made him feel a little safer. For some reason he felt the demon would strike only at someone who was alone. He thought about the teahouse girl who had received the golden-crane kimono from Umae. Had the demon killed her *because* of that? Thinking that the girl was, in fact, Umae? Then why did the bearded samurai return it? And who was the geisha who wore it at the silk maker's shop where the fire had started?

Suddenly he forgot about these questions. He looked down the street to the Teahouse of the Falling Cherry Blossoms. The lanterns Seikei had lit earlier had been extinguished by now. But someone was moving furtively along the front porch, as if he were trying not to be noticed.

It was no demon. Or if it was, it was a thief, not a murderer. For the skulking figure was dressed in the very same outfit that Seikei wore—the plum-colored jacket and pantaloons that had been stolen when Seikei washed them that afternoon!

Seikei broke into a run, trying to see the face of the thief, who had his back turned. Just before Seikei reached the teahouse, however, he saw a tongue of flame lick the underside of the porch. Then another, and another.

The figure in the plum jacket threw a burning stick down and then leaped over the railing. "Fire!" Seikei shouted. "Stop him!" he called out. He started to chase the thief, but then realized his first duty was to save the teahouse and those inside.

The front door was latched, but instead of waiting for someone to open it, he burst through the paper-and-pine frame. "Fire!" he called out. He rushed down the corridor, bumping into a large vase that stood on the floor. Clumsily he groped his way to the kitchen and filled a bucket with water.

He reached the front door only to find that others were already trying to put out the flames. Among them were the three samurai he had passed earlier, suddenly sobered by the sight of Edo's most dangerous enemy—fire. They were stamping on the flames. Seikei poured water on the place where the fire seemed worst.

By the time he came back with a second bucket, the

doshin had arrived as well. He jumped down from his horse and with a hooked steel *jitte*, he pulled burning parts of the porch away so the fire wouldn't spread.

"Don't let him get away," one of the samurai said. Seikei realized the man was pointing to him. Seikei held up the bucket as if to say, Look, I'm putting the fire out. But as he turned to go back inside for more water, the samurai grabbed him by the shoulder. "We saw him," he told the doshin. "He was the one who started the fire."

10—
WAITING FOR THE TORTURER

*S*eikei was humiliated. Uncomfortable too, but he told himself that didn't matter. A samurai must be willing to endure any hardship to serve his master. Judge Ooka had sent him to the teahouse to help solve the mystery of who was setting fires in Edo. Seikei was obliged to follow the path wherever it led.

Right now, it had led him to the courtyard of the local magistrate, Odozo. Seikei had been chained to a post by the doshin and left there for the rest of the night.

No one had listened to his explanation. Even though they should have seen he was trying to put out the fire, the drunken samurai had confused him with the real criminal. The doshin had taken their testimony as the truth. After all, there were three of them against Seikei's lone voice.

Odozo was not the sort of magistrate who liked to have his sleep disturbed. "You'll stay there till His Honor is ready to examine you," the doshin told Seikei.

"And if you want him to be lenient, you'd better keep quiet till breakfast."

"When will that be?" asked Seikei. He wanted to be released as soon as possible so he could look for the person who had set the fire.

The doshin only laughed. Seikei had tried to sleep but was unable to. Hours later, the sun had risen, the roosters had crowed, and birds were flying overhead. As yet, there had been no signs of movement within the magistrate's house. Nor were there sounds of activity in the street beyond the wall, as there certainly would have been by this time in Edo or Osaka.

At last a door slid open and a face peered out. It was a boy of about nine. He gave Seikei a curious look and then emerged, carrying two night jars. He emptied the contents into the privy and then addressed Seikei solemnly: "They say you're the demon."

"No," Seikei replied firmly.

The boy looked disappointed. "I hoped you were. I've never seen a demon. What did you do, then?"

"Nothing," said Seikei.

"Oh, that won't work with Judge Odozo," the boy replied. "Better confess. He'll just torture you till you do."

Seikei knew that indeed many judges did that. But he felt certain that as soon as he was brought before Odozo, the magistrate would recognize him. He, at least, would believe the truth. Afterward, Seikei would give him a report for Judge Ooka on what he'd learned so far.

In a little while the boy brought him a bowl of brown rice and a cup of water. "When does Judge Odozo come to examine the prisoners?" asked Seikei.

"When he feels like it," replied the boy. "The day starts late here in Yoshiwara."

That much was true, Seikei thought. Not until the sun had risen high in the sky did anyone else appear. Then two doshin, both holding their jittes as if they expected Seikei to attack, released him from the post he'd been chained to. Leaving his legs shackled together so that he could hardly walk, they took him by the arms and dragged him into the house.

Seated on a pedestal above the floor was Judge Odozo. He was studying a scroll but looked up when the doshin appeared with Seikei. He gave no sign of recognition.

The guards forced Seikei onto his knees. "You are accused of setting fire to the Teahouse of the Falling Cherry Blossoms," Odozo said sternly. "Do you confess to this crime?"

"I do not," said Seikei. "Someone else who was dressed in the teahouse clothing set the fire. I tried to put it out."

"Who might this person be?"

"I don't know. Someone stole the other set of clothes yesterday afternoon after I washed them."

The judge was silent for a while. Seikei looked up. "Don't you recognize me?" Seikei asked. "Judge Ooka sent me to the teahouse. He told me I could send reports to you."

He saw at once it was the wrong thing to say. Judge Odozo's face grew dark as a winter sky. When he spoke again, it was in a voice filled with ice. "Judge Ooka told me that I was to be more vigorous in my pursuit of criminals. He seems to think that certain deaths that have occurred here in Yoshiwara were crimes, not merely accidents. How he concluded this, I have no idea. I do not think he comes here often enough to know."

Seikei hung his head, trying to look respectful. He had an uneasy feeling that the judge was not going to set him free.

"It is true," Odozo went on, "that Judge Ooka told me to send him any reports you brought to me. But I have received no reports. Perhaps you found some other way of sending them."

Seikei opened his mouth to reply, but the judge silenced him with a look. "The only report I received—even before I had my breakfast—is that you attempted to set fire to the teahouse. There were witnesses to this. From the description the doshin gave me, I knew it must be you."

Judge Odozo smiled, pleased with himself. "You see, as clever as Judge Ooka is reputed to be, there may well be other magistrates just as clever." He thought this over and added, "Even cleverer."

Now Seikei hung his face not merely to appear humble. He was afraid his scorn would show.

"So it occurred to me," the judge went on, "what if Judge Ooka had planted a criminal right here in my district? With the purpose of testing me, so to speak? Perhaps even to make me look incompetent, if I did not see what was right under my nose?"

Seikei had to restrain himself from shouting at the man's stupidity.

"But now I have discovered what you were really up to," said Odozo with satisfaction. "So, do you wish to confess?"

Seikei took a deep breath to convince himself he was able to speak. "I did not set fire to the teahouse," he said very clearly.

Judge Odozo seemed offended that his cleverness had not broken Seikei's will. "Take him back to the prisoner's post," he said to the doshin. "Let him contemplate his errors until the torturer arrives."

Seikei felt as if he were having a terrible nightmare. Ever since he was a boy, he had been taught to respect the shogun's officials. He never expected to face one as unjust and arrogant as this man.

As the two doshin shackled him in the courtyard, he began to worry. He had heard gruesome stories about the tortures inflicted on criminals. Of course, since Judge Ooka didn't approve of torture, Seikei had never witnessed it being used. Right now, he understood the judge's reasoning: An innocent person might confess to a crime he did not commit, merely to escape the pain.

He shook his head to chase the thought away. To confess would be a cowardly act. He promised himself he would never dishonor himself in that way. But the thought remained in the back of his mind: Could he really hold out, if he were tested?

For a long time he sat there on the ground, wondering what he could say to convince Odozo he was innocent. There was no shade in the courtyard, and Seikei grew thirsty.

He saw the boy peeping at him from the doorway again, and motioned to him. The boy edged over, clearly trying to stay out of Seikei's reach.

"Could you bring me a cup of water?" Seikei asked.

The boy shook his head. "Not allowed to," he said. "Not till after you've been tortured."

"Have you seen anyone tortured?" asked Seikei. "What is it like?"

The boy's eyes clouded as he remembered. "The torturer is very strong. He's the biggest man I've ever seen, except maybe for *sumo* wrestlers. He carries an iron rod, longer than I am tall and almost as thick as my arm." He held his arm out so Seikei could compare.

"What he does is beat people with the rod on the bottoms of their feet. Well, you'd think that wouldn't hurt so much. You'd imagine you could endure that. But after five or six strokes people start to scream and beg him to stop. They can't help themselves, you see."

"I'd rather not hear any more," said Seikei.

The boy shrugged. "They give you a chance to confess after you start screaming. In any case, the torturer must stop after two hundred blows of the rod. That's as many as he is allowed to do in one day. It's the law. But I've never seen anybody go that long without confessing."

"No one?"

"No, I'm sure of it. That's why you might as well confess now and spare yourself."

"But I didn't do what I am accused of."

"Well, everyone says that, of course. What exactly did they catch you doing?"

"Setting a fire." Seikei caught himself. "But it wasn't me! It was someone dressed like me."

"Odd," said the boy, "that the two of you just happened to be there at the same time."

Seikei was struck by an idea. That must be the connection between the fire in Edo and the dead girl. The person who started the fire in the silk seller's shop was wearing the kimono taken from the dead girl. It had been Umae's kimono. Was the fire-starter trying to put the blame on Umae?

Seikei turned restlessly, feeling the tight shackles on his legs. If only he could tell Judge Ooka what he'd learned from the two geishas.

There were still other parts of the mystery to solve. How did the kimono fall into the hands of the bearded samurai? Why did he bring it back to Umae? And was any of this connected to the deaths of the other two geishas?

The boy was still talking. Seikei didn't want to listen. "Of course, the penalty for deliberately starting a fire is to be burned alive, and that might be as bad as the torture. . . ."

A shadow fell across Seikei's face. It was a relief in one way, for it shielded him from the sun. Then a second, frightening thought occurred: Perhaps the torturer had arrived.

Seikei looked up, but his eyes couldn't make out the tall dark figure who stood between him and the sun.

Then the figure spoke: "So this time the judge leaves you for only a day and look what happens. I receive word that a fire has been set in Yoshiwara, and who do I find is accused of it?"

"Bunzo!" Seikei said. His words filled Seikei with shame, but his presence gave him hope. "You have to believe me. I am not guilty of starting the fire."

"Oh, I know that," Bunzo said. "But you are guilty of letting yourself be disgraced."

Seikei looked down. "Do you think the judge will be

displeased with me?" He could endure anything but that.

Bunzo grunted. "Probably not. He seems to have a blind spot where you're concerned." He stooped down to Seikei's level. "In fact, he'll probably be angry with me if I don't get you out of here."

"Do you think you can do that?" Seikei asked.

"Judge Odozo and I have already talked. When I asked him where the witnesses to your crime were, he admitted he'd never seen them."

"They were samurai on the way home," Seikei said. "They probably went back to Edo."

"And you did not confess, did you?"

"No, I wouldn't do that."

"He would have when the torturer arrived," said the boy, who was listening intently.

"Bring the key and release him," Bunzo commanded.

"Judge Odozo has not—" the boy began, but Bunzo took a threatening step toward him and he ran off.

"When I told Judge Odozo that you were Judge Ooka's son, he saw his mistakes more clearly," said Bunzo. "If you want, he will apologize. I am sure of it."

"No, I just want to get out of here," said Seikei. "I have much to tell you."

UMAE'S CHOICE

*B*unzo took Seikei to a noodle shop and ordered a meal. Seikei was hungry, but between bites he explained what he'd learned so far. "Judge Ooka wanted to find the person who wore the kimono to the silk seller's shop," he told Bunzo. "It wasn't the dead girl. The kimono was taken from her. I think the reason was to get revenge on Umae."

"And this latest attempt to set a fire," said Bunzo, "do you think it is connected with the other fires?"

"It must be," said Seikei. "Whoever is doing this has some link to Umae. And that is her new teahouse. They may have wanted to burn it merely because she had been there."

"But in Edo," Bunzo said, "the fire-starter appeared to be a geisha. Here, it was someone who looked like you."

"I know," said Seikei. "It's puzzling, but I'm sure the judge can figure it out."

"Perhaps you should come back with me," said

Bunzo, "before you get into more trouble. I cannot always be expected to come to your aid."

Seikei's face flushed. "No," he replied. "The judge assigned me to work at the teahouse. I have more to find out there."

"Use caution," said Bunzo. "I would not like to have to inform the judge that your body was found in the river."

Seikei thought of the girl he'd seen in her coffin the day before. He would not like Bunzo to find him like that either.

They parted at the street that led to the boats. Seikei wondered how he would be received at the teahouse. Last night, the residents had seen him dragged off, accused of having tried to burn them alive. That surely would not have pleased Oba Koko.

It was dusk and once more the lanterns in front of the teahouses were being lighted. Like multicolored fireflies, the flickering lights hovered softly over the street as a lamp-lighter at each teahouse stretched his candlestick high. Seikei hurried a little, remembering that was *his* job. Even though he was there only to investigate, he didn't want someone else to do it.

Just as he came in sight of the house, however, the front door slid open. Seikei saw the tip of the pole used to light the lanterns. Then the rest of the pole, and finally the person carrying it.

A person dressed just like Seikei, in the plum-colored jacket and pantaloons of the teahouse. The only difference was that this person's outfit was fresh and clean.

Seikei broke into a run. The boy carrying the lighting pole turned and saw him. Dropping the pole, he turned and fled, just as he had the night before.

This time, however, Seikei did not hesitate to follow. Nobody in the teahouse was in danger. The other boy was thinner than Seikei and moved fast. But Seikei was stronger and within a few strides began to gain on him.

Glancing over his shoulder, the boy saw he was losing the race. He ducked into a narrow space between two teahouses. Seikei followed without breaking stride.

At the far end of the alley, a ladder was leaning against the wall. Passing it, the boy gave it a shove and it toppled toward Seikei. He had to jump back to avoid it. Then it blocked his path and he had to hop between rungs to get past.

By the time he reached the rear of the building, the boy was nowhere to be seen. Seikei searched behind some barrels and outbuildings but had no luck.

He had been close enough to see who his quarry was, however. It was Kiru, the boy who had lost his job the day Seikei had arrived.

And almost certainly it was Kiru who had stolen the set of clothes Seikei had hung up to dry. That meant he had to be the person who set the fire last night.

Seikei was excited by this discovery, but couldn't decide what it meant. Was Kiru the person who had set the fires in Edo? It seemed doubtful. And whether he had any connection to the person who did . . . Seikei shook his head. It was too bad Kiru had escaped.

Seikei walked back to the teahouse, out of breath from the chase. He found the lighting pole was still lying on the porch. The candle had gone out when it fell. Seikei was just picking it up when Oba Koko came outside looking as if she could use a broomstick.

"Lazy boy!" she cried. "You've been out here all this time and the lanterns are still not lit."

Then she recognized him. "You're not Kiru," she said.

That seemed obvious, so Seikei said nothing.

Oba Koko began to look around. "What have you done with him? Let him go at once. If you have enchanted him, I'll . . ." She stopped and looked sideways at Seikei. "I thought you said you weren't a demon."

"Oba Koko, Kiru ran away, that's all," said Seikei. "I didn't cast a spell on him. He was the one who tried to set fire to the teahouse last night."

"Is that so?" she said, looking at him with one eye shut. "I heard it was you."

"No, I was falsely accused, because Kiru was wearing the same teahouse clothes as I was."

Oba Koko nodded slowly. "Yes, that's so. He had them on this morning when he asked for his old job back. Where is he? I'll make him wish he'd been taken to the magistrate's house for the torturer."

"He's gone. He ran when he saw me coming."

"Hm. I guess he should have." She looked at Seikei suspiciously but shrugged. "I need *one* of you for tonight. If Kiru is not here then it must be you. But light the lanterns. It is already dark."

Seikei went to the kitchen to relight the candle on the end of the pole. The cook raised her eyebrows when she saw him.

"I am back," said Seikei, hoping she would have no questions. As he poked the end of his stick into the fire, he asked, "Will Umae be here tonight?"

"We have been told that she will be," said the cook. "Oba Koko and Nui went to visit her this afternoon."

"Nui too?"

"She can be very charming," said the cook. "I believe Umae will announce that she is taking Nui as her little sister." The cook paused. "So we all hope nothing will happen to disturb Umae tonight."

Seikei knew that remark was directed at him. "I will be careful," he said.

As he lit the lanterns, he gazed up and down the street. Customers were already arriving in Yoshiwara—younger, less wealthy men for whom the trip was an adventure. He saw boys not much older than himself, nudging each other and trying to work up the courage to go inside one of the teahouses. The bearded samurai would have stood out in this crowd. If he returned tonight, he would come later.

Umae arrived and was warmly welcomed by Oba Koko and Nui. Seikei stayed out of the way, but once he felt the geisha's eyes fall on him when he carried a barrel of sake past the party room she was using. Fortunately, the sight of him caused her no uneasiness; perhaps she had forgotten who brought her the kimono the night before.

Her favorite guests soon made an appearance. Jugoro and Genda showed up first. Seikei noted that each had brought a wrapped gift for Umae. The two men looked at each other with what Seikei thought was jealousy. Both had the same desire: to win Umae's special regard.

Oba Koko had apparently failed to persuade Maiko and Odori to return. In their place, she had invited two other geishas of lesser talents. They were willing to risk spending an evening in the same teahouse as Umae. It would advance their reputations.

However, many of the ordinary guests resisted being seated in the rooms with the lesser geishas. Last night's episode had, if anything, only increased Umae's popularity. Just as people ate the fugu fish even though it could be deadly, so too did the danger of a demon heighten the thrill of seeing Umae.

A generous gift of "thank-money" to Oba Koko won admission for several men who had not been in Umae's room last night. Thus, when the old daimyo who had spoken to Seikei appeared, the room was full. Seikei was at the front door and tried to steer the daimyo to one of the other rooms. But he insisted on going to Umae's.

All at once, Oba Koko was at Seikei's elbow, hissing at him furiously. "That's Lord Iwakuri," she said. "Find a place for him wherever he wants."

"But Umae has too many people . . . ," he explained.

"Do as I say!"

It was impossible to argue with her, so he led Lord Iwakuri down the hallway. Sliding open the door, he saw that Umae was in a happier mood tonight. Jugoro and Genda were seated on either side of her again, and she was singing a song about a girl torn between the man her parents have chosen for her and the one she loves in her heart.

The presents lay on the low table in front of her, still unopened. Ten or twelve other men in the room were enjoying the spectacle of watching the handsome samurai and the shogun's official wonder which of their gifts she would open first.

Seikei managed to find a place at the foot of the table for Lord Iwakuri to sit. The men on either side must have recognized him too, for they courteously moved aside to make room. The old daimyo needed help lowering himself to the floor, and held Seikei's arm for support.

"Sit behind me," Lord Iwakuri said, and Seikei obeyed. He was glad to have an excuse to stay there. If anything further happened to Umae, he wanted to be close by.

Umae handed her samisen to Nui and stood up. While the younger girl played a simple accompaniment, Umae danced and sang. Everyone else in the room sat silently, entranced. Umae could herself be a demon, Seikei thought—although one of a beautiful and delicate kind. Her arms seemed made of flowing water, not flesh, as she beckoned the guests to follow her on a trip to an unfamiliar world. With tiny steps and a soaring voice she led them to a place where love reigned supreme.

The story of which she sang ended like many others. The girl was forced to abandon her love and follow the path of duty. She married the man her parents had chosen for her. But her life was dull and filled with drudgery. Her husband showed her no tenderness. Then her lover began to send her notes. She met him secretly late at night. They declared their love and ran away.

But of course their time together was short. They had broken the rules that society had set, and thus there was no place for them to go. The only way they could be together was to die together. That was the path they chose.

Umae sank to the floor as gracefully as a falling

cherry blossom. The story ended. The lovers had killed themselves.

Why did so many people enjoy the love-suicide stories, Seikei wondered. Could it be that secretly they were dissatisfied with their own lives? He remembered how long he had yearned to be a samurai and not a merchant's son. How foolish a dream that had been! Yes, through a miracle, it had come true. But few could hope to succeed as he had.

Seikei wondered if, in time, he would have been content with the fate that had seemed destined for him. He looked around the room. All these men had their own roles to play—lives that were determined by duty. A few, he suspected, were merchants. Even though most were wealthy, was it possible that they were dissatisfied too?

After resting for a moment, Umae rose and resumed her place at the table. Everyone offered compliments on her skill at dance and song. Genda poured her a fresh cup of sake and Jugoro offered her a particularly nice morsel of eel.

"I am happy to have pleased you," she said. She politely filled the cups of the other men at the table, including the old daimyo, Lord Iwakuri. He took an extra cup and handed it to Seikei. Seikei tried to refuse, but Lord Iwakuri insisted.

The liquid was sweet and bitter at the same time.

Seikei had tasted sake before, and knew that this was of high quality.

At last Umae turned her attention to the presents. "Which should I open first?" she asked in a teasing voice. "I cannot decide."

Genda and Jugoro were both too proud to urge her to decide in their favor. But the others at the table made loud suggestions as to which appeared to be the better gift.

Finally, Umae called Nui to her side. "Nui will blindfold me," she said. "And then mix up the gifts so that I cannot tell which is which. The first one I touch I will open."

The old daimyo reached to refill his cup while Nui was preparing the blindfold. He turned to refresh Seikei's as well. Finding it still nearly full, he said, "Come now! You have to drink faster than that!"

Seikei realized Lord Iwakuri had mistaken him for a guest. He politely downed the rest of the cup and held it out. "This is just like Umae," Lord Iwakuri confided as he filled it. "You'd think she'd be grateful to receive two gifts. Instead, she will make those two fools feel like they weren't generous enough. I used to bring gifts for her myself. But nothing ever satisfies her. She may sing beautifully of suicide, but she drove at least one man to kill himself."

Hoping to hear more, Seikei took another sip of the

sake. But everyone's attention was diverted to the head of the table, where Umae was now choosing. Nui mixed the presents and put them within her reach. Blind-folded but smiling, Umae fluttered her hands like butterflies seeking a place to land. Finally they floated down and rested on a wrapped box. Seikei could see by the look on the two men's faces that it was Jugoro's.

12—
A WARNING IGNORED

Jugoro's smile lit up his face. Seikei thought that Umae must have preferred him over Genda anyway, for Jugoro was by far the more handsome man. Genda was trying to accept the decision with good grace, but his tightly closed lips showed that it was an effort.

Umae had removed the blindfold and now held up the present for all to see. "Open it," the other guests urged her. Now that the first part of the game was over, they wanted to comment on the merits of the present.

Slowly, drawing out the suspense as long as possible, Umae untied the thin silk ribbon that enclosed the box. She slid off the rice-paper covering without tearing it. Finally she lifted the lid.

Inside was another box—far more beautiful. This one was made of wood covered with many shiny coats of black lacquer. Over that base was painted a rural scene with flying birds and small animals. After showing it for admiration once again, Umae opened it. Inside was a writing set—brush, ink stick, inkstone, and sheets of fine paper.

Umae expressed her delight at such a generous gift. She praised Jugoro's taste in selecting the perfect present—something that she would always treasure.

Seikei was impressed by her acting ability. For he saw that the writing set—though suitably expensive—was in fact quite ordinary. Growing up as a merchant's son had taught Seikei the difference between what was truly fine and what was merely showy. This writing set could have been turned out by any competent crafts worker. Even the paper was ordinary—made for business, not for a memorable gift.

The other guests now urged Umae to open Genda's gift. Perhaps they, like Seikei, suspected that it would put Jugoro's to shame.

But Umae set the writing set down and folded her hands. "First," she said, "I want to announce something. I wish to share my joy with you."

Those around the table seemed to become more alert. This was a surprise, and they all looked at each other to see if anyone knew what it was going to be.

Only Seikei had an inkling, for the cook had told him earlier.

"I want to declare formally," said Umae, "that I have accepted Nui as my new younger sister." She gestured toward Nui, who tried to lower her eyes modestly. Seikei could see, however, that for her it was a moment of triumph.

"From now on," Umae continued, "Nui will be at my

side to learn. I will guide her in the arts that geishas know."

The guests politely congratulated Umae. Of course it was Nui who should have received the congratulations, thought Seikei. But while Nui was a younger sister, she was obliged to display obedience, humility, and deference to others. That might be difficult for her, Seikei thought.

Then Umae astonished everyone. She picked up the remaining present, the one Genda had brought for her. "Since from now on everything I have will be Nui's to share . . . I am giving her this gift."

Seikei heard a few sharp breaths from the guests around the table. As Umae handed the present to Nui, all eyes went to Genda. He was, naturally, enraged, but honor demanded that he not show it. He smiled as if this were exactly the way he expected his present to be received. But Seikei noticed that Genda wiped the palms of his hands on his kimono.

Nui was delighted, but remembered to display modesty. She protested that she was unworthy of such a gift—all the while letting her eyes flick from guest to guest, gauging the effect of her performance.

Finally Umae urged her to unwrap the gift. When it was revealed, Seikei thought that Umae had chosen the right man, but the wrong gift. Genda's present had been selected with care and taste, not just money. It was a porcelain tea bowl decorated with plum-tree blossoms. Seikei recognized it as the work of Kenzan, a famous potter known to be so shy that he seldom spoke to anyone. It was said that he broke most of the things he created because he considered them imperfect. Genda must have gone to a great deal of trouble to obtain the bowl.

Nui thanked him profusely, but everyone could see that Genda would much rather have had Umae's gratitude. The bowl was passed around the table so everyone could examine and praise it. Jugoro was particularly gracious in his admiration for it. Seikei wasn't sure if he really understood how much better Genda's gift was than his own.

Lord Iwakuri refilled Seikei's cup again. "You see," he asked, "how foolish it is to try to please a geisha?"

"Yes," Seikei said. It was a lesson Nui had already taught him. Then he remembered something that the woman who had hired the priest had said. The teahouse girl who had drowned—she had received the kimono from Umae as a gift. Perhaps she had even been killed for that very kimono.

And now it was Nui who had received a gift from Umae. Seikei suddenly felt very uneasy. Should he warn her? Would she take him seriously?

He had to try. But the old daimyo was still talking and Seikei couldn't get away. "Some men do not profit from seeing the mistakes of others," Lord Iwakuri went on. "Even if it comes within their own families. It was his brother, you know. The one who killed himself out of an uncontrollable desire to please Umae."

Seikei was watching Nui closely. She was still trying to imitate Umae's alluring gestures. When Umae laughed, Nui laughed. When Umae playfully suggested a game, Nui clapped her hands. Yet she had much to learn, Seikei thought. She might have been more beautiful than Umae, but the geisha had skills that had been polished over many years.

The old daimyo stood up. He was a little unsteady, so Seikei rose to help him. Seikei nearly slipped, finding that he was feeling the effects of the sake too. "I am tired," said the daimyo. "I have had enough for tonight." He tottered out the door, leaning on Seikei's arm. "Remember," said the daimyo, "do not betray your honor by letting your heart follow its desires."

"I won't," Seikei assured him.

Oba Koko appeared. "Aiii, Lord Iwakuri," she cooed, "I hope you are not leaving."

"I have already stayed too long," he replied, taking a few silver mon from a pouch in his sleeve. He pressed them into her waiting hand. "Can you call my kago-bearers?"

"They are waiting for you," she replied. "Nephew!" she commanded in a sharp voice as if Seikei hadn't been paying attention. "See to it that Lord Iwakuri rests comfortably in his kago."

"Yes, Oba," said Seikei. He helped the old man to the

doorway. Two kago-bearers stood in the street at the bottom of the steps. Between them was the comfortable passenger-box that Lord Iwakuri had arrived in.

Seikei helped the daimyo step inside. As Lord Iwakuri settled back on the pillows, Seikei suddenly recalled what the old man had said earlier. "Whose brother was it that killed himself?" he asked. "Out of passion for Umae?"

The daimyo looked at him. "I thought you knew. It was that man at the head of the table." He rubbed his forehead. "His name escapes me. You know . . . the one who brought the gift."

Seikei had no chance to ask more. One of the kago-bearers slid shut the door and they were off.

He slapped his head for not paying more attention earlier. The brother of whoever killed himself over Umae would certainly have a reason to hate her.

But then Seikei considered further. Lord Iwakuri must have meant either Jugoro or Genda. Those were the two who brought gifts. And neither seemed to have the slightest feelings of ill will toward Umae. On the contrary, they were competing for her affections. The old daimyo must be mistaken, understandable considering how much warm sake he had drunk.

Seikei still wanted to warn Nui about accepting a gift from Umae, but now he had no excuse to return to the party. In fact, as soon as he went back inside the teahouse, Oba Koko had a job for him. Someone in another geisha's room had spilled a jug of sake and he had to clean it up.

The rest of the evening was uneventful. Seikei wondered if the bearded samurai would make an appearance, but he did not. One by one the guests departed. Seikei saw both Genda and Jugoro leave, which signaled the end of Umae's party. Not long afterward, Umae's kago-bearers arrived. Naturally, both Nui and Oba Koko knelt at the front door, expressing their gratitude for the great honor Umae had bestowed on the teahouse.

Seikei came forward as soon as the kago had left. "Nui," he said, "there's something you should know about the gift."

"Oh," she said, "I knew I shouldn't have left it in the room. You've broken it, haven't you?"

Oba Koko looked in their direction, and Seikei instinctively held his hand up to protect his nose. "No," he said. "The tea bowl is perfectly safe. It's you who are in danger."

Nui looked at him, and for a second he thought he did see fear in her eyes. Then she laughed. "I don't believe that nonsense about you being a demon," she said. "You can't frighten me."

"But there *is* a demon," he said, "or anyway, a criminal who acts like a demon. At the last teahouse Umae went to, she gave a kimono to one of the girls. Her name was Akiko. She was drowned because of that kimono, I'm sure of it."

"What of it?" said Nui. "I'm not going to be wearing the tea bowl. If *someone*," she said, staring at Seikei as if he were the someone, "wants to steal it, he will have to take it from the teahouse. And Oba Koko will catch him. And this time, Judge Odoro won't let him go."

"But there's more to it than that," Seikei explained. "I think Akiko was killed because she was close to Umae."

"I think you are merely jealous of my happiness," Nui retorted.

"No, that isn't it—" he began, but she had turned her back on him.

"Enough of that," Oba Koko commanded. "Out in the courtyard with you now so I can latch the kitchen door."

Seikei shrugged. He had no other choice—and, of course, no proof that his suspicions were true.

Oba Koko gave him no candle or lantern to take to the sleeping hut. Of course not, for either one might start a fire. In the darkness he unrolled the sleeping mat. He was glad to remove the teahouse uniform, which he'd been wearing for a day and a half. Wearing only his *juban,* an undershirt that reached to his knees, he lay down.

He expected to fall asleep at once, but the events of

the past three days swirled through his mind. At the heart of it all was the bearded samurai. Of that, Seikei was sure. But catching him was another matter. Ruefully, Seikei admitted that he could not even catch the person who stole his clothes.

Seikei decided to use a mind-relaxing exercise that Bunzo had taught him. He concentrated on the night sounds he could hear through the walls of the hut. As he identified each one, he forced himself not to hear it. The goal was to reduce all the noises to silence, and then sleep.

A party was still going on in one of the teahouses behind this one. It would soon end, he thought. Someone was emptying a pail of dishwater in a drain farther down the courtyard. A couple of crickets were chirping, trying to find each other. And somebody not far away was crying.

13—
THE THIEF'S STORY

Seikei sat up from the sleeping mat. There was no doubt about it. Although the sound of the crying was muffled, he heard it clearly now that he concentrated on it.

He couldn't tell for sure, but he imagined it must be a girl or young woman. The thought of going to her rescue made him feel bolder. If he couldn't solve the mystery or catch the demon, Seikei could still become a hero in someone's eyes.

He opened the door to the shed and looked out. The moonlight was enough to give him a good view, but he couldn't see the person who was crying. He took a step, listening carefully.

The crying stopped for a moment, as if Seikei's footstep had been noticed. Then he heard it again, only this time it sounded as if it were coming from another place.

He hesitated. It was possible that someone, or something, was trying to lure him into a trap. He had a sudden vision of the form he imagined demons took—with claws, long fangs, and eyes that blazed red in the darkness.

Seikei shook his head. He reminded himself of the code of the samurai: A samurai is willing to face death without fear. He made himself take a step forward. Instinctively he reached for the wooden sword he usually carried under his obi. But he had left it, days ago, at the gatehouse.

Some firewood was stacked against the wall of one of the teahouses. Seikei saw that some of the logs had been pulled aside to make a space big enough for someone to crawl inside. He saw a pair of white *tabi* socks in the darkness. He leaned over . . . and then saw the plum-colored pantaloons that matched his own.

With a cry of triumph and anger, Seikei grabbed Kiru's feet and dragged him out of the hiding place. "You won't get away from me this time," he said.

Kiru's voice came as a whimper. "Don't hurt me." He rolled over and put up his arms to shield himself. Seikei could see that he wasn't going to put up a fight. But Seikei held tight to the boy's feet anyway, remembering how fast he could run.

"What are you doing here?" Seikei asked. "Planning to try to burn down the teahouse again?"

"No, no," said the boy. "I'm sorry I did that. I just . . . I had no place else to go. I thought I could sleep in the shed, but now they've given that to you too."

Seikei frowned. "It's not that grand," he said. "It

hasn't even got a window. You could find someplace else to go."

"No, I can't," the boy insisted. "I wanted my job back. I would have gotten it back, if you hadn't come along just then. Oba Koko has fired me lots of other times. But I would just wait outside until she needed something done."

"But you would never have gotten your job back if you'd burned down the teahouse."

"I know that. I'm not stupid, you know. Or anyway, not *that* stupid."

"So why—"

"The basket woman told me it would work. She said if I started the fire, I could put it out when everybody rushed downstairs. Then I'd be a hero. That's all I intended to do. But then you came along again and chased me away. So I thought *you'd* be the hero. Why did the doshin take you away?"

"Some samurai saw you setting the fire and thought it was me," Seikei told him. "That was because you were wearing the same clothes. It was you who stole them, wasn't it?"

"Yes. The basket woman told me to."

"Who is this basket woman?"

"She sells medicines and charms. She carries a basket full of them. People go to her if they can't afford a regular doctor."

"Or if they want something that will hurt an enemy,"

Seikei said. In Osaka, where he grew up, there were people who sold such things too. His father the merchant told him they were unreliable, but worth a try if all else failed.

"Yes," admitted Kiru. "I went to her for a charm to get rid of you. That was when she suggested I steal the clothing."

"And she was the one who told you to set fire to the teahouse?"

"Yes."

"Where is she now? Where does she live?"

"I don't know." Kiru shrugged. "People say she comes here from Edo. She said that if I set fire to the teahouse, people would say you did it and I could get my job back."

"How could you get your job back if the teahouse burned down?"

"Oh . . . she promised me she would cast a spell on it so it really wouldn't burn. It worked too. I got my job back. But then you chased me away a second time. Why did you do that? You can't really want this job. I can tell you've had an education."

"Never mind," said Seikei. "Where can I find this woman?"

"I don't know. When I went to the place where I promised to meet her, she wasn't there. I hoped she'd have another idea on how to get rid of you."

Seikei almost laughed, but his mind was racing. Now he had several more things to tell Judge Ooka.

"Do you know how to get to Edo?" he asked Kiru.

"Of course. You ride the boat. Everyone knows that. You do think I'm stupid, don't you?"

"No, but I need your help. Could you take a message to someone? His house is in the Marunouchi district, near the castle. I'll give you directions."

Kiru hesitated. "Ahhh . . . would you pay me?"

"Pay you?" Seikei was incensed. "You're a criminal. I should have you thrown into a jail."

"Well, let go of my feet and I will try my best."

Seikei could see Kiru was lying. "Tell me something," Seikei said. "After you get off the boat in Edo, which direction do you go to reach Marounichi?"

"Ummmm . . . that way?" Kiru said, pointing vaguely in a direction that had no meaning at all.

Seikei hammered Kiru's feet on the ground in disgust. "You have no idea, do you?"

"Well, the truth is I have never been to Edo," said Kiru. "You only asked me if I knew how to get there."

"You haven't been to Edo? Have you always lived here in Yoshiwara?"

"For as long as I can remember. My mother was a geisha, but when she died, I had to go to work."

Seikei sighed. "Come on, then," he said. "I'll show you what Edo looks like. I'll have to take you to the judge myself."

Kiru wasn't sure he wanted to go. Seikei had to

promise that Judge Ooka wouldn't punish him. "He'll be grateful for this information."

"How grateful?"

Seikei caught on. "Not grateful enough to reward you," he said. "But I can assure you of one thing—if your information proves helpful, you can have your job at the teahouse back."

"Really?" Seikei could hear the skepticism in Kiru's voice.

"Yes, I give you my word."

"What will you do then?"

"I will make myself disappear."

"Ahhh," Kiru said, nodding. "I would like to see that. Or not see that, after it happens."

Seikei got dressed and they went through an alleyway back to the main street. Soon they were on the boat headed downstream, along with several customers returning from Yoshiwara.

Seikei had retrieved his wooden sword, which had still been at the gatehouse where he left it. Kiru looked at it warily. "You're not supposed to carry a sword."

"In Edo I can," said Seikei. "The rule against swords applies only in Yoshiwara."

"I thought only samurai could carry them."

"My father is a samurai," replied Seikei.

Kiru thought this over. "Why were you working in a teahouse then?"

"You'll learn that later." Some of the other samurai on the boat seemed to be listening to this conversation. Seikei didn't want them to challenge his right to carry a sword.

"I'm not stupid, you know," said Kiru.

At the landing in Edo, kago-bearers waited to pick up customers who needed help getting home. Many did. But Seikei decided he and Kiru could walk to the judge's residence just as easily.

The streets were dark and silent. All ordinary citizens had gone to bed hours before. The houses and shops were all shut tightly. Anyone who wished to use the night for pleasure—whether in teahouses or kabuki theaters—had to go to Yoshiwara.

There was little to fear from thieves, because Edo had almost no crime. Punishments were harsh, it was true. But a more important reason was the one the judge had pointed out to Seikei: "A criminal chooses to disrupt the proper order of society. Everyone realizes that is dangerous to all, so few indeed will hide or protect a criminal."

Even so, there clearly was at least one criminal at large in Edo. Seikei silently asked the kami spirits for protection from that person, be he human or demon.

To reach the judge's home, they had to cross one of the many moats protecting the castle. Seikei led Kiru onto the narrow wooden bridge that spanned the water.

Halfway across, Kiru stopped. "I don't want to go any farther," he said.

"What? Why not?"

"It's too big here. I was curious about it, but now I've seen enough. I want to go back."

"You can't go back," Seikei pointed out. "You don't know the way."

Kiru looked around. They had indeed traveled through a maze of small lanes and wide boulevards that curled around the city. Yoshiwara had only five streets and all were laid out in a rectangle. You couldn't get lost there.

"I'll just stay here till daylight," said Kiru. "Then I'll find my way back."

"That won't work," Seikei said quickly. "Just before dawn, the shogun's doshin round up everyone on the streets. They assume that if people have no homes, they must be criminals."

"Is that true?"

"Do you want to wait and find out? Or come with me? It's not much farther. We can be drinking tea and eating hot *soba* in a little while."

"Soba? Noodle soup? You aren't lying to me, are you? Because you know, I'm not—"

"I'm not *lying*," Seikei interrupted. "Come on, hurry up."

Reluctantly, Kiru followed.

As one of the shogun's officials, the judge had been given a grand residence in the area closest to the palace. Unlike most of the ordinary houses of the city, its walls were of stone that had been transported down the river from a quarry. It was two stories high with an overhanging red tile roof that shielded it from the sun. In the back, Seikei knew, was an elaborate stone garden where the judge went to clear his mind. As Seikei and Kiru approached, it looked as if everyone were asleep. The doors were shut tight and there was no sign of a light.

However, just as their feet touched the bottom of the steps to the porch, the front door suddenly slid open. Bunzo stood there, his hand on the hilt of his sword. He nodded when he saw Seikei and then looked quizzically at Kiru.

"I recognize those clothes," said Bunzo. "Is this the criminal who tried to set fire to the teahouse?"

"I thought you said—" Kiru began to protest. Seikei grabbed his arm to stop him from running away, and spoke to Bunzo. "It is, but he has important information for the judge."

Bunzo gave Kiru a look that even frightened Seikei. "Anyone who sets fires must be severely punished."

Seikei tightened his grip on Kiru. "Let us in, Bunzo. The judge can decide. I gave my word as a samurai."

Bunzo grunted, not favorably.

14—
THE TEMPLE OF KANNON

The judge took somewhat longer to appear than Bunzo had. Seikei wondered if Bunzo ever slept, but there was no doubt that the judge did. By the time he joined them, the cook had arisen too, making tea and, at Seikei's request, steaming bowls of soba. The judge sat down on the floor with Seikei and Kiru.

"I see you have brought me important information," he said.

"I *think* it's important," said Seikei.

"If it were not, you would not have brought this boy and you would not have awakened me," the judge pointed out.

Seikei nodded. He hoped the judge would agree that Kiru's story was important. The judge calmly ate his bowl of soba, slurping noisily to show his enjoyment, as Kiru repeated the story he had told Seikei. Seikei had to supply details at a few points.

When Kiru had finished, the judge thought for a few moments. Finally Kiru worked up the courage to break the silence. "Can I have my job back now?" he asked.

The judge glanced at him. "Not just yet," he murmured. He looked at Seikei. "What happened last night at the teahouse after Bunzo left you? Did the bearded samurai return?"

"No," Seikei said. "Umae announced that she was taking Nui, one of the teahouse servants, as her little sister." He went on to tell the story of the two gifts.

"Umae gave Nui the better gift?" asked the judge.

"It seemed that way to me."

"She must have high regard for her. In that case, you should return there immediately and keep the 'little sister' in your sight at all times."

Seikei wondered how he would accomplish *that*. "You see the connection," the judge went on. "Those who are close to this Umae are in peril of their lives. The two other geishas, the woman who was drowned in the river . . . Now we know the *why*."

"Revenge on Umae?" said Seikei.

"Yes, but the *who* is not apparent."

"The bearded samurai?" suggested Seikei.

"It seems likely," agreed the judge. "But we do not know his real name. Do not forget the woman selling medicines and charms and urging others to start fires. I would like very much to ask her some questions."

"I'll go find her for you," Kiru volunteered.

"No," the judge said. "You will remain here as my guest while Seikei returns to Yoshiwara."

Kiru looked around as if suddenly realizing he'd

been trapped. For a moment, Seikei thought he would try to run again, but Bunzo, standing by the doorway, shook his head and Kiru's shoulders slumped.

"You gave your word," he said to Seikei.

"I meant it," Seikei told him. He turned to the judge. "There was one other thing I learned." He described what Lord Iwakuri had told him about the man who had killed himself. "So either Genda or Jugoro would have had a reason to hate Umae. But I don't believe it."

"Why not?"

"Because both brought gifts for her. They seemed . . . in love with her."

The judge smiled. "One may give a gift with one hand to draw attention from the knife in the other. This is valuable information. I will have a talk with Lord Iwakuri." He yawned. "But not now. Be on your way, so that you will return to Yoshiwara before daybreak."

"No one rises there at daybreak," Seikei told him.

That was true. And by the time he reached the teahouse, Seikei was exhausted. He closed the door of the shed, lay down on the worn-out sleeping mat, and fell asleep immediately. Because the shed had no windows, the sunrise did not awaken him. Nor did the noises of activity that began later as the other residents of Yoshiwara were starting their day.

In fact, it was not until Tsune rapped on the door of the shed that Seikei opened his eyes again. "Is anybody in there?" she called. "The cook wants you to grate *daikon* roots, whichever nephew you are."

Seikei staggered to his feet and opened the door. The bright sunlight nearly blinded him.

"You look terrible," Tsune commented. "Nui told Oba Koko that you were drinking sake with the guests. Too much of that will give you a headache."

Nui's name reminded Seikei what he should be doing. "Where is she?"

"Oba Koko? She's at the carpenter's shop. One of the guests fell through a door last night."

"No, I mean Nui. Where is she?"

"Oh, she and Umae went to Edo. Umae is going to present her at the Temple of Kannon."

A chill went through Seikei. "What?"

"Yes, that's the custom when a geisha takes a new little sister. Kannon is the special Buddhist saint of the geishas, because they believe she is all-loving and forgiving. It's in Asakusa, in the northern part of the city."

"I know where the temple is," said Seikei. "How long ago did they leave?"

"Oh, quite a while. They were going to make a holiday of it. The district around the temple has many amusements. I wish someone would take *me* to a . . . Where are you going?"

While she was talking, Seikei had put on his real clothes, the ones he wore as a samurai's son.

"To Edo," he said.

"You can't do that! I'll have to grate the daikon. Oba Koko will be angry. You'll lose your job!"

"Tell her Kiru wants it back," he said over his shoulder as he hurried off.

He had disgraced himself for certain this time, he thought. The only instruction he'd received from the judge was to keep Nui in his sight. And what happened? Seikei fell asleep, allowing Nui to get away.

Sleep was treacherous. Seikei had once asked Bunzo how he managed to get by without sleeping. Bunzo replied, "Sleep between times of watchfulness." As far as Seikei could tell, Bunzo meant he could sleep and be on guard at the same time—something Seikei clearly had not mastered.

So now he had to return to Edo on the boat. He retrieved his sword at the guard station, but as he tucked it into his obi, he had a feeling he was unworthy to carry it.

Just when Seikei wanted to move fastest, the world seemed to be going slowly. At this time of day, there were almost no customers leaving Yoshiwara. The boatman delayed his departure, hoping for more passengers until Seikei gave him extra money to start at once. Even then, the pilot let the current of the lazy River Sumida carry the boat at its own pace.

Finally the boat docked, and Seikei rushed toward the Asakusa-bashi Gate, the eastern entrance to Edo. By this time of day, a throng of people had gathered in front of the gate. There were riders on horseback, kago-bearers, and dozens of travelers on foot; some were laborers carrying tools, others were people bringing goods for sale. All were in a hurry to get to wherever they were going.

Passing through the gate, Seikei soon entered a very different neighborhood. He knew he had arrived in Asakusa simply by observing the people who passed by. They were nearly all women and children.

As the headquarters of the shogun's military government, Edo was dominated by men. There were about twice as many men as women living in the city.

But in Asakusa, that proportion was reversed. Women and children filled the streets. They had come here for the entertainments, the shops, and the countless diversions—many of which required no money at all to enjoy. Seikei wanted to move quickly, but his path was continually blocked by the crowds that gathered to watch jugglers, sword swallowers, acrobats, wrestlers—anyone who hoped to earn a few coins from the audience.

Over every shop hung a banner advertising the products within. These included anything that could be used to make women beautiful: cosmetics to enhance eyes, lips, and cheeks; eyebrow tweezers and pencils; nail polish; gorgeous combs and hair ornaments; and *yoji* to beautify the teeth by blackening them. For children, stalls offered candies, fruits, and toys such as kites, tops, balls, dolls, and miniature animals made of paper.

Amusement stalls were everywhere. As Seikei made his way through the crowds, he was accosted by barkers encouraging him to pay a coin or two to enter a booth and see wondrous things: strange animals brought from China or the barbarian lands, contortionists who could tie their bodies in knots, a man with six fingers on each hand, a goat with two heads.

Finally Seikei found his way into a large square. It too was filled with people, but at the heart of it he could see the Temple of Kannon, rising high above the confusion and clamor below. Supposedly the temple had stood here for more than a thousand years, although because it was made of wood, much of it had been rebuilt over the centuries. The sound of hammering indicated that even now carpenters were hard at work keeping it new.

Seikei ascended the broad wooden stairway from street level to the platform where the temple itself stood. The front portico was painted with shining red lacquer, as were the immense pillars that held up the sloping roof high overhead.

There were no doors. Seikei, along with scores of other pilgrims, simply walked between the wooden pillars into the great hall where the ancient gilded statue of Kannon stood. Dressed in flowing robes, she held in front of her a jewel resting on a lotus leaf. Many believed this represented the gift of enlightenment.

According to legend, two fishermen had pulled the statue from the nearby river in their net. Not knowing who it was, they threw it back. But the statue returned again and again. Finally they took it to the local daimyo, who recognized it as Kannon and built a shrine on the spot.

Kannon had shown a special power to help women and children. The geishas therefore had adopted her as their patron. Each new geisha came here to make an offering and ask the blessing of holy Kannon. Older geishas had their own favors to ask. So did women with children or those about to become mothers. They too brought gifts, hoping that Kannon would watch over them in childbirth and protect their children from harm.

Seikei searched the faces of the crowd, looking for Umae and Nui. Each time he saw a geisha, his heart filled with hope, but none turned out to be Umae. As he drew closer to the image of Kannon, however, he saw something he recognized. There, among the offerings that had been left today, was the exquisite ceramic tea bowl. Genda would have been surprised to see that the gift he had so carefully chosen for Umae had ended up here.

Seikei found a monk who was helping some of the

older women ascend the steps to the image. "Have you seen a geisha and her little sister? They were bringing a tea bowl to offer to Kannon."

"I must have seen them," the orange-robed monk replied. "But among so many . . . I could not tell you one from another."

"Where would they go after making the offering?"

The monk gestured outward toward Asakusa. "Many people find something here to distract themselves from their worries," he said.

Feeling helpless, Seikei made his way back down the steps that led to the noisy streets below. Where would Umae have taken Nui to celebrate?

All at once, he saw Umae's face in the crowd. She caught his eye at the same time. As he rushed forward, he saw the anxiety in her eyes. She was alone, and even before she spoke to him, Seikei knew what had happened.

15—
UMAE'S SECRET

*W*here is Nui?" Umae asked him. "What have you done with her?"

Seikei was astonished that she asked *him* these questions. "I was told at the teahouse," he said, "that the two of you came to make an offering to Kannon. I followed because—"

"The temple!" said Umae. "Yes, perhaps she's gone back there. We must go and look."

"I just came from there," Seikei told her. "Umae, please, tell me what happened. Where did you last see Nui?"

Umae rubbed her hands together. Seikei could see she was trying to calm herself. "When she disappeared . . . I thought . . . I thought of the demon people have been talking about. I feared it was you because no one had ever seen you in Yoshiwara before and you brought me the kimono. It frightened me because it was the one I gave to Akiko. Did you know that?"

"I learned it," said Seikei. "But the kimono didn't

come from me. It came from the samurai who called himself Fukushu. Do you know who he really is?"

"No. I didn't understand why he gave that name— Revenge."

"But tell me about Nui. Where did she go?"

Umae made another effort to gather her thoughts. "We decided to look at the horses of Kannon. The monks keep two milk-white horses for her to use when she returns in human form. Their stable is behind the temple. But on the way there, Nui saw a woman selling charms."

"Charms?"

"Yes. You know, something that they promise will bring you good luck or health or riches. They're supposed to have good kami within them."

"Was this the same woman who sells charms in Yoshiwara?"

"I don't know."

Seikei's mind raced. "How did she—what happened?"

"Well, dear little Nui said she wanted to buy something for me. I guess Oba Koko gave her some money in case she needed it. So the woman said she would take her to a shop where Nui could get something special. Nui told me to go on to the stables and she would meet me there. She wanted to surprise me. But I waited and waited and she did not appear."

Nui was foolish, Seikei thought. She would have allowed herself to be tricked into going someplace else. "Take me to the place where you met the woman," he told Umae.

As they made their way to the rear of the temple, Seikei blamed himself again. Now the worst had happened—and all because he had been sleeping while he was supposed to be on guard.

"It was here," Umae said. They stood in a narrow street where the shops specialized in articles for those who wanted help from the spirit world. Some sold gifts guaranteed to please Kannon. Others offered prayer beads and prayer wheels; sacred texts that brought benefits even if one couldn't read them; and relics such as saints' bones, hair, fingernails, or objects that a holy person had touched.

Seikei took Umae into each shop, where she described the woman who had taken Nui away. Most of the shopkeepers merely shrugged. Like the monk, they had seen too many people for anyone to stand out.

At last, exhausted, the two of them entered a small shop that sold tea and rice cakes. Umae was trained to conceal her emotions, but Seikei could see she was under a great strain.

"I must tell you," he said after they sipped some tea, "that Nui's disappearance is my fault. You must not blame yourself." As the geisha's startled eyes met his, he added, "No, I am not the demon. But Judge Ooka entrusted me with protecting you and Nui, and I have failed."

"I do not understand," Umae said. "Why would such a person as Judge Ooka be concerned about a geisha and her little sister?"

Seikei told her about the fire and the geisha who had been seen in the silk merchant's shop. "That is what brought us to Yoshiwara. There we saw the funeral notice for Akiko, and learned that she had been wearing a kimono like the one the silk merchant saw."

"My kimono," said Umae.

"So it seems."

"But I was not the geisha who started the fire in the silk merchant's shop. I seldom leave Yoshiwara at all. Before today . . . aii, I wish I had not left there today. Kannon did not smile on us. Poor Nui."

"But you see," Seikei told her, "all of this has a connection to you. Who would have reason to try to harm you? Who wants revenge? What have you done?"

Umae sat silently thinking. Seikei could see no expression on her face. "I am only a geisha," she said finally. "My life is spent trying to please men, not anger them."

Seikei felt she was concealing something. "Even so, I have seen you offend people."

"Have you? When was that?"

"Last night, when you gave Genda's gift to Nui. Genda was displeased by that. And when you saw his gift . . . you must have regretted it, for it was much finer than Jugoro's."

She smiled slightly. "You noticed that, did you? You have good judgment. Shall I tell you a secret?"

"Anything that will help me find Nui."

"I do not know if it will. But perhaps. I knew beforehand that Genda's would be the better gift. Jugoro is young, handsome, but has no appreciation of the finer things. Genda is an experienced man. When I sing or dance, he is the person whose compliments mean the most to me."

Umae took the teapot and refilled Seikei's cup. He could not help but notice how delicate and lovely she made the act of pouring tea seem. She noticed his gaze and smiled at him. Seikei's face grew warm. He felt the allure that drew so many men to Umae. He suddenly knew that he wanted his compliments to matter the most, to have Umae dance for him alone.

The spell was broken as he listened to her continue the story. "So," she said, "I had arranged secretly with Nui that she would put Jugoro's present where my hand would fall on it, even though I was blindfolded."

"What?" Seikei was bewildered. "Why—?"

She fluttered her hands gracefully. "Nui needed something to sacrifice to Kannon today. She could not herself afford a suitable offering. I gave Genda's gift to her for that purpose. But, sadly, Kannon does not seem to have been pleased."

Seikei was openmouthed with astonishment. "But didn't you worry about what Genda would think?" he asked.

She looked at him. Her large, beautiful eyes were full of mysteries that he would never solve. But this one she chose to reveal. "You are young," she said. "You may know the difference between a fine tea bowl and an expensive but vulgar piece of pottery. But you do not know men. Probably you will never know men as well as I do. Genda will respond to my inconsiderate treatment of his gift by bringing me a better one next time—one so good that I cannot ignore it."

For a moment, Seikei couldn't breathe. He saw at once that she was right, but at the same time he realized how much smarter Umae was than the men she dealt with. Could Nui ever understand men that deeply? He thought not.

Seikei shook his head. He had fallen under Umae's spell, but none of this was helping to find Nui. "Someone told me . . . I must ask you . . . did a man kill himself because of you?"

Umae's expression did not change, but Seikei felt as if her eyes had turned cold. "Who told you that?"

"It doesn't matter. But is it true?"

She continued to stare at him. "There are men who think they can buy geishas. And, in truth, some geishas are willing to sell themselves. A woman has few choices in this world. A woman must obey her father, and do what he decides. If her father sells her, she must accept the life he has chosen for her. If he selects a husband, she must of course marry him. Afterward, she must please and obey that man as if she loved him dearly."

Umae leaned closer to Seikei. He could smell the delicate perfume she used, and her nearness frightened him. "If a geisha works very hard, she can save enough money to repay what her father received for her. Then, she can earn for herself. Some would say she is free."

She leaned back and sipped from her teacup to calm herself. Seikei noticed that her hand was shaking slightly. "And once free," she asked, "would you sell yourself a second time?"

She waited for an answer, watching him. He thought of one: "Did someone try to buy you a second time?"

"Every night," she replied, and laughed. It was a bitter laugh. "*That* I agree to, but one man wanted me to be his alone. I could leave Yoshiwara, he said. He would buy me a grand house in Edo, with servants. I could live as well as the wife of a daimyo."

"He wanted you to marry him?"

"I see you do not understand," Umae said with a sad

little smile. "Unfortunately, he already had a wife. It was not a wife he wanted, but someone who would be a plaything."

"And you refused."

"Yes, but he thought he could sway me with presents." Umae's eyes turned away from Seikei and back to those memories. "The gifts became more expensive, more numerous. I accepted them, of course, because I am a geisha and must live on the generosity of men. But no matter what he spent, every gift only showed what a vulgar man he was. Not like his brother."

Seikei nearly jumped. "His brother? Who is his brother?"

"Genda."

Genda! Seikei tried to understand what that meant. Now he knew who the bearded samurai—but no, it couldn't be Genda. Genda was at the teahouse at the same time as the samurai who called himself Revenge.

"Was the bearded samurai Genda's brother, then?" he asked.

Umae frowned. "No, of course not. It was just as you said. Genda's brother killed himself. People said it was because of me, but . . ." She trailed off.

Seikei's mind reeled. "Then why does Genda—" He couldn't finish the question.

But Umae understood. "He comes to my parties because he loves me too."

Seikei stared at her. He had never met anyone like

Umae, so heartless, so calculating. She was as much a demon as the person who set the fires.

Then he remembered what the judge would say to him: "Now we know the *why*. *Who* is becoming clearer."

"I must go," said Seikei.

"Did something I said help?" Umae asked. "Are you going to find Nui?"

He hesitated. "I don't know, but now I know where to look."

16—

THE EYES OF THE DEMON

*S*eikei had been to Genda's house once before, when he had delivered some official papers for the judge. It was surrounded by a wall of packed earth, shielding it from the eyes of passersby. That was a shame, Seikei thought, for the house was impressive. It consisted of two large two-story sections, connected to each other by a one-story entrance hall. As far as Seikei remembered, one side of the house was used for Genda's official duties and the other was for entertaining and sleeping.

Seikei was surprised to find no guard at the front gate. Indeed, when he passed through, he saw no sign that anyone was at home. Of course, he realized, Genda himself probably had duties to perform at the shogun's castle. Maybe Seikei's journey here had been in vain. Now that he thought about it, he probably should have gone to the judge's residence first and told him what had happened.

But that would mean Seikei would have to confess his carelessness at losing Nui. If he could find her by himself, it might lessen his disgrace. In fact, perhaps he could solve her disappearance in a way that might make it unnecessary for Seikei to mention his disgrace at all.

He went to the front door of the main hall and pulled the bell cord. He heard it ring somewhere inside. After that, the only sound was the chirping of locusts in the hot sun. No one responded either to the bell or to the locusts.

Seikei could hardly believe the house was deserted. Maybe it was only his imagination, but he sensed that someone was waiting for him to leave. He walked around to the side of the house. A little path of flat stones had been built here. He followed it through two rows of tall, graceful cypress trees that stretched high above, hiding the house.

Beyond, he entered what seemed to be a scene from the countryside. On a placid lake, a line of ducks left ripples in the water. Lily pads, some with pink flowers open, clustered near the banks of the lake. Purple and yellow irises bloomed along the shore.

Surrounding the lake were large stones—carefully placed, Seikei knew, to look as natural as possible. As his eye ran across them, he realized that one was not a stone at all. It was a woman in a gray kimono, seated with her back to Seikei. He might indeed have mistaken her for a rock or a statue except that she turned her head slightly when she heard his footsteps.

She looked so peaceful that Seikei hesitated to disturb her. He took a few steps farther and then stopped. Finally the woman rose and turned to face him. "I was not expecting a visitor," she said.

The woman was middle-aged, but wore a jet-black wig that contrasted with her sagging cheeks and heavy chin. She lowered her eyes to the ground, as if she were a servant.

"I am Seikei, son of the samurai judge Ooka Tadesuke," he said. He spoke formally, hoping to impress her.

She bowed and replied softly, "My name is Suzu. When I saw you just now, I was surprised, for I had seen you earlier in Yoshiwara. You did not seem like a samurai's son then."

Seikei was flustered. He couldn't remember ever seeing this woman, and he wasn't sure he should explain what he was doing in Yoshiwara. "I regret that my visit is unexpected," he said. "But I have an urgent message to deliver to Ometsuke Genda."

"From Judge Ooka?"

Seikei hesitated. "In a way," he said. What a stupid thing to say, he thought. The woman must think him a fool.

"Ometsuke Genda is not at home," she told him. "Would you like to leave the message with me?"

"No, it . . . requires an answer. An immediate answer."

"In that case, you will have to wait. I expect O-Genda

to return soon. Would you care to have some tea while you wait?"

Relieved that she was allowing him to stay, Seikei accepted the offer. While she went inside the house, however, he started to worry. Perhaps it was unwise to come here without telling the judge first. He wanted to find Nui, of course. But everything seemed so calm and peaceful here. She must be somewhere else, and he should be going.

What would he say to Genda anyway? What would Genda's response be if Seikei said, "I know your brother killed himself because of Umae. Therefore you must know where Nui has disappeared to." It was ridiculous. Seikei would be fortunate if Genda only laughed at him, instead of taking grave offense. At the least, Seikei would only embarrass the judge and disgrace himself further.

The woman named Suzu returned with a tray holding a pot of tea and cups. Perhaps, Seikei thought, he could get some information from her. He waited until she sat and poured tea for each of them. Taking his cup, he expressed gratitude and sipped a little tea.

The taste was interesting. As the son of a tea merchant, he had learned to identify teas from all parts of Japan. But this was new to him. Intrigued, he took a second, longer sip.

"I don't recognize this tea," he said. "It is quite good."

"I blend it myself," she said. "It has sweet herbs in it. You'll find it relaxing."

That was true. He enjoyed the feelings of peace and calmness that spread through his body. It seemed like the first time in many days that he was able to rest.

Then he caught himself. No, rest wasn't what he came here for. He must stand now and walk around.

But as he tried to get up, something strange happened. The house seemed to turn on its side. Seikei puzzled over it for a moment. Then he realized it was not the house, but he who had toppled over. He was lying on the soft ground, and had spilled the tea.

The tea. He realized too late that the tea was what had caused him to become relaxed. So relaxed that now he could no longer move.

A face appeared in front of him. It was the woman, only now her eyes looked directly into his. He recognized them, and then fear took hold of him. Intense hatred blazed from them, the same hatred that he had seen in the eyes of the bearded samurai.

"I was afraid you would recognize me," the woman said. "But you didn't expect to see *me*, did you?" She slipped off her wig. Underneath, her real hair was cut in the style of a male samurai.

She was indeed the samurai, the one who called himself Fukushu. But that was impossible!

The woman put her finger under her nose and wiggled it. "Oh yes," she said mockingly. "If a woman can add eyebrows to her face, she can add a mustache and even a beard."

She took hold of Seikei's collar and pulled him upright. "It really is a pity you have found me," she said. "You disturbed my meditation. I was sitting here preparing myself to set fire to my brother-in-law's house."

Slowly, she dragged Seikei across the paving stones. He could hear and see, but no matter how much he willed his body to obey, his arms and legs were useless.

"Genda would have lost the house in any case," Suzu continued. "In pursuit of that demon Umae. He is as big a fool as was my husband, his brother." She stopped to rest, and looked down at Seikei. "I wonder if you found out about my husband. Perhaps that is what brought you here. But you couldn't know the disgrace, the shame that his suicide brought to me and my children. If he had any honor left at all, he would have killed us too."

She looked back out at the lake. "It was all the fault of the geisha. She bewitched my husband and now has bewitched Genda too. Did you see that tea bowl? The one that is now at the Temple of Kannon? It was *my* gift."

Her eyes blazed. "I chose it and my husband bought it for *me*. It was the only thing I had left from him. Genda took it from me to make up for the fright I gave Umae when I returned the kimono. He punished me by taking away the bowl, which he knew I cherished. He could do that because now I must live in his house, on his charity. Obey his orders, like a servant. That is the way it is with women."

She shook her head. "I think I will stay a man from now on."

Seikei thought of Umae and wanted to tell Suzu that they were very much alike. But he could not speak.

Suzu lifted Seikei by the collar again. "But first, I must dispose of you and leave the final clue that will make everyone believe it was Umae all along—that it was she who started the fires."

She dragged him up the steps to the back door of the house. Seikei struggled to make his voice work, to argue with her. Nothing but a gurgle came from his mouth, but she heard it and knew what it meant.

"Yes, I know, you are the son of the mighty Judge Ooka. His adopted son, I hear. Genda told me who you were. No doubt the famous judge will be saddened to think that Umae brought you and her little sister here, to the house of her wealthy and powerful patron. For Judge Ooka will discover your bodies and conclude that in her jealousy and madness, Umae set fire to the house."

No, Seikei thought, the judge will not be fooled. He will find you and punish you, for you are describing yourself.

The calmness induced by the tea took possession of Seikei. He had solved the case, and the judge would know it. His duty was fulfilled. It seemed not really to matter that he was about to die. This must be the way a true samurai feels, he thought, when he faces an enemy in mortal combat. He closed his eyes.

17

IN THE FIRE

*W*hen Seikei awoke, he was in a room he didn't recognize. The walls were covered with paintings of battles and armored samurai. In one corner stood a shrine to Hachiman, the war kami. Hachiman's fierce image glowered down at Seikei as if to remind him of his duty.

Seikei tried to get up. He realized that feeling had returned to his arms and legs. Unfortunately, now they were bound with strong cords.

He heard a noise and rolled onto his side. There, on the floor on the other side of the room, was Nui. She too was bound with cords.

She looked angry. Right, blame me for this too, thought Seikei. Fortunately, a gag kept her from speaking. Even so, she murmured something underneath the gag.

Seikei understood what she meant: "We're in trouble. Do something."

Slowly he recalled what the woman named Suzu had told him. "How long have we been here?" he asked Nui, but of course she couldn't answer.

His hands were tied behind his back. He pulled at the cords as hard as he could, but that was useless. After several tries, he managed to sit up so he could look at the cord that bound his feet. The knot was securely tied. He wouldn't be able to slip out of it.

Then he smelled something that caused a chill to run through him: smoke.

Nui noticed it at the same time, and her eyes grew wide with fear. "Um mmnm chmm nnun!" she said as loudly as she could, banging the back of her head on the floor for emphasis.

There was no doubt about it. Suzu was carrying out her plan to burn down the house. Seikei looked around frantically, and his eyes lit on the one thing that might help them. On a wooden stand in front of Hachiman's shrine rested a curved *katana,* the longer of the two swords that samurai carried. It was sheathed in a scabbard of exquisite design. Seikei was sure that the sword itself must be in excellent condition.

If so, that meant it was so sharp, it could cut a man's body in half with a single blow. Or, if Seikei could manage to unsheath it, it would slice the cords that bound him.

He wiggled in that direction, only to lose his balance and topple onto his side again. Nui was doing her best to shriek for help under the gag, but Seikei was sure Suzu was the only other person in the house. She must have sent the servants away so no one would notice the fire until too late.

After a few more tries, he found it was easier simply to roll across the floor. Nui stopped making noises long enough to stare at him. It was clear that even if Seikei rolled to the door, he couldn't open it.

Seikei bumped into the dark wooden stand, finding that it was heavier than it looked. Shifting position, he raised his legs and pushed it. The stand wobbled slightly. He gathered his strength, propped his back against the floor, and pushed again. This time it toppled over with a crash.

Hoping that Suzu was too busy to pay attention to the noise, Seikei rolled to where the sword had fallen. To his dismay, it was still snugly resting in its scabbard. He worked his way to a sitting position again, turning his back to the sword. His fingers were still numb from the tea and from being bound. But at last he managed to get a grip on the hilt of the sword. Awkwardly, he drew it part of the way out of the scabbard.

He reached with his other hand, attempting to hold the scabbard still. Instead, he felt the edge of the sword slice into his fingers.

Nui, who could see what he was doing now, gave a cry of warning or fear. The sword was so sharp that Seikei barely noticed the pain of the cut, but he could feel his blood trickle down his palm.

He coughed, nearly losing his grip on the sword. The smoke had grown worse. It was visible now in the room, drifting from somewhere else in the house. Seikei felt the air grow warmer, and could hear the crackling of flames too. Hurrying as fast as he could, he leaned backward, trying to push the cord against the edge of the blade.

Once more he only succeeded in cutting himself, this time on the soft pad at the base of his right thumb. Ignoring the pain, he shifted position slightly. The next time he leaned back, he felt the pressure of the blade, but not on his hand. He felt the binding loosen. Then he twisted his hands sharply and was free.

When he brought his hands around in front of him, the sight made him feel sick. He remembered how he'd felt the first time he'd seen someone cut the head off a chicken. Dizzy, he put his head between his knees and closed his eyes.

Then he heard Nui, mumbling more frantically than ever. He couldn't lose consciousness, he told himself.

He grasped the sword and cut the cords that bound his feet. Shakily, he stood up. He wasn't sure if he could even walk. But in a few moments, he had freed Nui as well. As soon as he loosened the gag over her mouth, however, she said, "Be careful! You'll get blood on my kimono! It's my best one too."

"Let's get out of here," he muttered. "The house is on fire."

"It was that woman," Nui explained. "She brought me here, telling me that I would meet someone who wanted to be my patron. And then she gave me tea that made me sleepy—"

"I know," Seikei said. "Hurry up." He slid open the door and smoke rushed into the room. Both of them started to cough. Stooping low, he went into the corridor and saw a stairway leading down. They must be on the second floor of the house. Taking Nui's hand, he led her to the top of the stairs, but a searing wave of heat drove them back.

"We can't go down that way," he said. "That's where the fire is."

"But there's no other place to go!" she shouted.

"Look for a window," he told her. There had been none in the room where the woman had tied them up. Crouching low to breathe clearer air, they found another door. Sliding it open, they saw daylight on the far wall.

They ran to the window and looked out. Just below them was the section of the house that served as an entrance hall. But they could not jump, for it too was in flames.

Seikei thought quickly. "We'll have to climb onto the roof," he said. "From there, we can find someplace where we can make our way to the ground."

"I don't want to," she said.

He glared at her. "It's either that or stay here and be burned alive," he told her.

She hesitated and looked out the window again. "You go first," she said.

Once Seikei stood on the window frame, he could easily reach the overhanging edge of the roof. Forcing himself to ignore the pain in his hands, he pulled himself up.

Lying facedown on the tiles, he reached back inside the window. Nui stared at his bloody hands, then closed her eyes and reached toward him. He clasped her hands and lifted. She wasn't as heavy as he feared. As he brought her onto the edge of the roof, her feet dangled over the flames below. Just at that moment, unfortunately, she chose to reopen her eyes and look down. She cried out in terror.

Suddenly another cry, louder and angrier, answered her from the opposite wing of the house. Seikei looked and saw Suzu's face at a window. He was glad she couldn't reach them, for she looked enraged at being cheated of this part of her revenge.

He had to ignore her for now, he told himself. The important thing was to get to some part of the roof where they could climb down to safety.

Just getting Nui to stand was an effort. "Don't look down," he told her. "Just imagine that you're walking on a tile floor." But she refused to walk. Finally, he had to settle for crawling with her to the peak of the roof.

From there they had what ordinarily would have

been a magnificent view. Now, with the house in flames around them, Seikei was only aware that the roof might collapse at any minute. He strained to see through the smoke, looking for a clear place below.

Then he heard the sound of horses' hooves. He turned in the direction of the road and saw several riders approaching. The size of one of them made it unmistakable who he was—Seikei's foster father, Judge Ooka. And right beside him were faithful Bunzo and Lord Iwakuri.

Straddling both sides of the roof peak, Seikei stood as high as he could and shouted, "Judge! Bunzo! Up here!"

They looked in his direction and waved. Urging their horses forward, they entered the front gate of Genda's mansion. For a moment Seikei lost sight of them. He turned and said to Nui, who was hugging the roof peak with all her might, "Everything will be all right now."

"Nothing can save us," she wailed. Seikei started to explain to her that the judge and Bunzo could accomplish any feat. Nui interrupted him with a scream that was even more piercing than before.

"There's no need for—" he began, but turned to see what she was pointing at.

He saw Suzu—no longer at the window, but on the roof. She seemed to have no trouble maneuvering across the hot tiles, and was rapidly closing the distance between them. Most alarming of all, she carried a katana that looked every bit as sharp as the one that Seikei had cut his hands on.

Seikei reached for his own sword. Though it was wooden, a master swordsman could use it to defend an enemy armed with a blade. He reminded himself of that, trying to forget the unfortunate fact that he was not a master swordsman.

His attention was distracted by shouts from below. Bunzo was motioning him to come to another part of the roof. Apparently the way down was clear there.

Seikei took hold of one of Nui's arms and pushed her in that direction. She resisted for a moment, until he said through his teeth, "Move, or I'll throw you off the roof myself."

She stared at him, astonished. But then she moved. Seikei went with her, looking over his shoulder. Suzu was nearly upon them. He let go of Nui and turned. He would have to fight the demon to allow Nui to escape.

He stood, balancing himself carefully with his legs spread wide in the defensive position. Suzu would be coming at him from higher up on the roof, so he prepared for a downward blow.

Behind him, he could hear Bunzo calling for Nui to jump. He shut those sounds from his mind and concentrated on Suzu's eyes, even more terrifying than before. Seikei willed himself not to fear. . . .

She struck downward with the blade, just as he expected. Holding his sword with both hands, he blocked her thrust. Turning to his right immediately, he avoided the sideways parry that Bunzo taught him usually follows a failed downward blow.

Now, Seikei and Suzu faced each other at equal height. With one foot farther down the roof than the other, both fighters were slightly off balance. Seikei considered an offensive strike, but decided to wait for Suzu's next thrust and parry it.

Suddenly he felt something catch hold of his lower foot. He could not distract himself by looking down, but he knew it had to be Nui. He tried to shake her off. "Let go!" he called, all the while keeping his eyes trained on Suzu.

A new expression suddenly appeared in the demon's eyes. Her burning hatred gave way to anticipation. She must have seen an opening where Seikei was not prepared to defend himself. As she turned slightly, he understood. Her next blow was going to be aimed at Nui, who was lying helpless at their feet, afraid to jump despite Bunzo's encouragement. If Seikei allowed Suzu to kill Nui, he could easily strike Suzu a decisive blow.

He could not do that. Suzu raised her blade with a triumphant look. Seikei thrust his own sword between her and Nui, hoping to block her.

And then a sound cut through the air like a swarm of bees, ending in a sickening thud. Seikei didn't understand what it was until Suzu cried out. He looked at her upraised arms and saw that an arrow had pierced both her wrists, holding them together like shackles.

The sword dropped from Suzu's hand and clattered down the roof. Enraged and baffled, Suzu took a step backward, slipped, and tumbled over the edge of the roof with a scream.

Dazed, Seikei looked down at the ground below. He saw Judge Ooka standing there, observing calmly as Bunzo and the other samurai rushed to where Suzu's body lay.

The judge was holding a bow in his hands. Seikei recalled his last lesson with Bunzo. Bunzo denied that he was a master of kyudo, the art of archery. Someday, Bunzo had told Seikei, he would see a real master and know the difference.

Now he had.

"Aren't you going to help me?" asked Nui.

18

A DEMONSTRATION
OF SKILL

The judge and the shogun were demonstrating their skills at kyudo on the practice field at the shogun's castle. Seikei had been invited to watch, although thankfully he didn't have to demonstrate *his* skills, because of the bandages on his hands.

Seikei soon saw that the judge wasn't really using his full skill. His arrows always hit the target just a little less accurately than the shogun's had. That alone, Seikei thought, showed how good an archer the judge was.

The shogun knew it too. "It is a shame," he chided the judge, "that however close I get to the heart of the target, your arrow is always there, just a hair farther away than mine."

"I always follow your lead," said the judge, "and my skill is evidently that small amount less than yours."

The shogun smiled. Seikei had heard people in the streets of Osaka and Edo say he never smiled. But they had never seen him with his friend and adviser Ooka.

"Let us rest," said the shogun. "I am tired of being humbled."

The judge bowed. "I will try to do better next time."

They sat on a little stone terrace that overlooked a particularly beautiful spot on the castle grounds. "I did not feel like having a formal tea ceremony today," said the shogun. "The demands on my time are too great. Still, I would like to hear how you solved this latest case." He looked at Seikei. "And once more with the help of your son. You must be placing him in danger just to impress me with his courage."

"I merely sent him to a teahouse," replied the judge. "He managed to put *himself* on the roof of a burning mansion."

Seikei's hands stung at that remark. His feet too. They had been burned on the roof tiles. He hoped the judge would not tell the shogun that he ended up on the roof because he overslept.

Servants brought tea and some of the cakes that the shogun knew the judge particularly liked. The shogun waited until the three of them had been served, then asked: "The burning roof . . . I understand that Genda's house was destroyed. Do you think he deserves additional punishment?"

The judge pretended to ponder the question. He had already told Seikei that Genda had often spread stories at the shogun's court, trying to ruin the careers of those he disliked, including the judge. "Even so," the judge had said, "if I take advantage of his current distress to ruin his name, I would disgrace myself and be unworthy of a position of trust."

So the judge told the shogun the truth. "Genda did not know about his sister-in-law's criminal activities. She has recovered from her fall, and has admitted that. Once, while Seikei was present, Genda saw her in the guise of a male samurai. He did not expose her true identity, but later he confronted her. She explained the disguise by saying she merely had wanted to see what the geisha Umae looked like. Genda did not suspect what else she was doing."

"I must say," remarked the shogun, "that this woman caused much trouble for others without harming her real target. If she chose to kill people, why did she not kill Umae and be done with it?"

The judge took another cake and sat back, contemplating its immediate disappearance. "Her reasoning was twisted," he said, "but understandable. Her own husband squandered his estate in a vain attempt to impress Umae. Reduced to poverty, he committed seppuku—embracing a samurai's death, even though he had lost his honor."

The judge began his assault on the defenseless cake. "When Suzu's husband killed himself," he went on, "he did not have the courage to kill her and their children.

Instead, he left them in poverty and disgrace. Genda took them into his home, but did not conceal his contempt for Suzu."

The cake crumbled, putting up no resistance. The judge swallowed, brushed his hands, and said, "Thus, Suzu wanted Umae to feel the disgrace she had felt. Death would have been too good for her. Suzu sought to make it appear as if Umae were cursed and that everyone near her would suffer. Thus Umae would be cast out of the only life she had known—as Suzu had been."

"But why the fires?" asked the shogun. He moved a tray of cakes toward the judge, putting them in desperate danger. "What was the point of trying to burn down half of Edo?"

"That too she hoped would reflect badly on Umae," said the judge, studying his quarry. "The silk maker who first set us on the correct path confirmed after seeing Suzu that she was the person who had set the fire in her shop. She told me something else that she concealed at the time I first questioned her. The silk for the kimono itself had actually been purchased in her shop."

"Is that so?" asked the shogun. "Then she must have known it was stolen."

"Not necessarily," said the judge. He poured tea for Seikei with one hand while slipping another cake off the tray with the other. Seikei had been so intent on the tea that he almost missed the abduction of the cake.

"The person who purchased the silk," the judge went on, "was Suzu's husband. He made a gift of it to Umae, who later gave it to Akiko, the girl who lost her life because of it. Knowing that, I have subsequently discovered a pattern. Suzu set each of the earlier fires in shops where her husband had bought gifts for Umae."

The judge picked up the cake with a look of deceptive affection. "She had a double motive: She wanted revenge on those who had contributed to her husband's downfall, and she left some token there that she hoped would lead to Umae."

"But no one discovered that pattern," the shogun said, "until I called you to investigate. You must stay here in Edo from now on."

"In truth," said the judge, who had now completed the obliteration of the cake, "finding the pattern earlier would only have led me to the wrong person. It was my son's observations that provided the key to the mystery."

The shogun looked at Seikei, who was blushing with pride. Seikei tried to appear observant, humble, and obedient. "You should have told the judge before you chased after the criminal yourself," said the shogun sternly.

Seikei knew better than to respond. He merely bowed his head in agreement.

"Actually," said the judge, "he was not chasing the criminal, but following my instructions to keep the servant girl Nui under observation. That led him to the criminal and into great danger. He might have overcome her by himself. However, I obtained the missing piece of the puzzle from Lord Iwakuri and arrived in time to help."

"I heard," said the shogun. "Lord Iwakuri told me yours was the greatest arrow shot he had ever seen. Too bad you never seem that skillful when you practice kyudo with me." He put the tray of cakes in front of Seikei, who took one for politeness' sake.

"Is the judge teaching you the principles of kyudo?" the shogun asked Seikei.

Seikei looked to the judge for guidance.

"Actually," said the judge, "his training is in the hands of Bunzo, who knows more about kyudo than I do."

"I doubt it," said the shogun. He turned to Seikei again. "But I am sure the judge has taught you about muga—clearing your mind of all distractions before you shoot."

"Yes," said Seikei. "I have had great difficulty with that." He looked at his hands. "But when I was fighting Suzu on the roof . . . I started to understand what it is all about. I forgot about my hands and focused on her."

"Good, good," said the shogun. "I will invite you another time—when you have solved another case, no doubt. Then you can demonstrate *your* skills. But the judge should teach you the secrets of muga himself.

Come now, Ooka, can you enlighten us? Recall just what you were thinking when you made that remarkable shot?"

The judge paused. "I knew the case was solved and that you would invite me to tell you how it was done. And so . . . I was thinking about how pleasant these cakes would taste."

AUTHORS' NOTE

Judge Ooka was a real person, a friend and adviser of Yoshimune, the shogun who ruled Japan from 1717 to 1744. For most of that time, Judge Ooka served as the city magistrate of Edo, the shogun's capital—a post that was similar to mayor.

Fires were a constant threat to Edo, and Judge Ooka devised ways to keep them from spreading. He divided the city into forty-seven sections, each of which had its own fire brigade. Watchtowers were built throughout the city so that if a fire broke out, the alarm could be sounded immediately. When that happened, firefighters came from neighboring sections to help the brigade already on the scene. Judge Ooka also enforced anti-fire building codes, such as having roofs built of tiles rather than wood or straw.

The judge's ability to solve crimes through his amazing powers of reasoning made him a folk hero. Many stories have been written about the man whom some call the Sherlock Holmes of Japan. This story, however, comes from the imagination of the authors.